THE 14th COLONY

The Struggles of a Young Frenchman
to Reach the Louisiana Colony

Kent Mayeux

A fictional account based on real characters
with a historical perspective
First book in a three part series

Kent Mayeux Publishing, LLC
Baton Rouge, Louisiana

Kent Mayeux Publishing, LLC
7937 Valencia Ct.
Baton Rouge, Louisiana 70820
www.newevangelization.net

Ordering Information:
Quantity sales. Special discounts are available on quantity purchases by
corporations, associations, and others. For details, contact the publisher
at the address above.

Front cover drawing is provided courtesy of the Norman B. Leventhal
Map Center at the Boston Public Library, Edward E. Ayer Manuscript Map
Collection.

Back cover map by JF Lepage, the copyright holder of the work under the
terms of the GNU Free Documentation License; From Wikipedia, the free
encyclopedia.

History sections provided from Wikipedia and the internet in general.
Interior book design and layout by www.intergrativeink.com

ISBN: 978-0-9823649-5-6 (paperback edition)
ISBN: 978-0-9823649-6-3 (ebook edition)

1. Drama 2. Action and Adventure 3. History 4. Trilogy

First Edition

About the Front Cover Drawing

The hand drawn map on the front cover was taken from the memoirs of Jean-François-Benjamin Dumont de Montigny (Dumont). His writings about French Louisiana include a two-volume history published in 1753 entitled *Mémoires Historiques sur la Louisiane*. In 1719, Dumont sailed from La Rochelle, France, to the Louisiana Colony, with a commission from the minister of marine as a lieutenant and engineering officer. Dumont was part of a unit of soldiers with orders to develop concessions (land grants) owned by a group of rich French investors including Charles Louis Auguste Fouquet, duc de Belle-Isle. Dumont lived in the colony for 17 years and permanently left the colony for France in 1733.

The drawing is provided courtesy of the Norman B. Leventhal Map Center at the Boston Public Library, Edward E. Ayer Manuscript Map Collection. The website description of the map says that it is a depiction of a plantation on Saint Catherine Creek in Natchez, Mississippi. However, further research indicates that the St. Catherine concession was located on Rivierre Blanche (White River later named St. Catherine Creek) while this front cover map clearly demonstrates its location on the Mississippi River.

The name of the plantation provides evidence of its true location in the colony. The caption of the map as translated from French reads "The Chaouachas Concession, formerly belonging to Monseigneur the Duc de Belle-Isle and partners." Duc de Belle-Isle served as Superintendent of Finances under King Louis XIV of France. His partner was Claude Le Blanc, Secretary of State for War for King Louis XV. Belle-Isle and Le Blanc owned several concessions in the Louisiana colony. One was the Terre Blanche concession on the

Rivierre Blanche (St. Catherine Creek) at the Natchez Post. They also owned a concession at the Yazoo Post. The map on the front cover of this book is a concession on the right bank of the Mississippi River, descending, across from and south of New Orleans. The name gives its identity away. Chaouachas was a small Indian tribe on the coast of Louisiana on the west side of the Mississippi River among whom this plantation was located.

The legend of the map as translated from French reads as follows:

"An Explanation of the figures

1. House of director
2. Kitchen (cooking)
3. Metal shop (forge)
4. Armory
5. Hospital (surgery)
6. Carpentry
7. Barn for cattle

8. Lofts (topped with a flag)
9. Chicken coop
10. Garden
11. Barn
12. Barn
13. Indigo

14. Dwellings of negroes
15. Their urinals (outhouse)
16. Pit
17. Running water (canals)
18. Levee
19. Landing (on the river)
20. Bell to call the negroes to work (topped with a flag)
21. Mission cross
22. Bridges
23. Cleared land (fields)

The Saint Louis River
(later the Mississippi River)"

Chapter One

April 1720
Village of Maintenay, Bishopric of Amiens,
Picardy Province, Kingdom of France

"Deliberate indifference, that's what I have been feeling from my father lately," said Pierre, as Simone tousled his curly brown hair. "I never feel the love I so desperately want from him. He has treated me differently from Nicholas and Emily, but I can't say exactly how. Father has been distant with his affection towards us but especially with me."

A tallow candle flickered on the desk in Pierre's bedroom. Simone listened intently while she lovingly stroked his hand. He confessed his emotional insecurity to her. They lay in Pierre's bed, with the bedroom window open. A light breeze from the cool spring night came inside and stirred the aroma of smoke from the candle around the room. Pierre was bothered by the smoke, but he was mostly overwhelmed by confusion. His mind wandered between the detachment he felt about his father's love and the affection he felt from Simone.

"Pierre, you have it so good here in Maintenay. Your father is the tax collector; you live in this nice house with your family; and your tutor has been wonderful. What more could you ask for? If only I were in your shoes."

"But I am just not satisfied," said Pierre. "Something is missing. Our profession is frowned upon, and the people of the province despise us tax collectors. I cannot picture my whole life living as Father does. The business is more and more demanding of his time, and Father makes less and less money."

"I love you so much," said Simone, as she leaned forward to kiss Pierre. She was petit and attractive, and well endowed at the age of fifteen. Her long black hair accented her muscular build and tanned skin, both of which she'd acquired from arduous physical labor in the fields with her mother and father.

"You shouldn't be here," said Pierre. "If Father finds us, you know how angry he gets with me. He might just kill us both."

Simone didn't care. She disrobed as she kissed Pierre and pulled on his shirt. Burdened by self-pity and lack of moral certitude, his uncontrollable sexual desires proved no defense to his base human nature. Pierre returned the affection. They slipped under the cotton sheets covering the old, feather-stuffed mattress, and Pierre made love to Simone. Sweat poured off their bodies. They took liberty with each another. They were both seeking something, but Pierre, at least, was not quite sure what it was. The candle flickered out as they fell asleep in each other's arms.

There was a pounding at the front door. Francois Mayeux, Pierre's father, rolled over in his bed, waking from a deep slumber. "Who in the hell is banging on the door at this hour of the morning? For God's sake, it is not light outside," he said.

He slowly got out of bed, feeling around for his night shoes. He complained to his wife, Marie, that he couldn't find the flint to light a candle. "Here's the son of a bitch," he said. After scratching on the flint for a second or two, a warm glow emerged from the candle enough to see his way around the house. He walked down the creaky stairs, and again heard the banging at the door.

"Let us in," someone commanded from outside.

"Who are you, and what do you want at this ungodly hour?" said Francois. He fumbled with the lock on the front door.

"I am Lieutenant Jean Claude with the royal guard. Let us in."

"Hold one moment." Francois slowly removed the bolt from the wooden door. He could only imagine what the royal guard wanted with him at this hour.

As he opened the door, the candlelight shone over an old lieutenant with a weather-beaten face, dressed in a royal blue uniform. Another guard was with him.

"Can I help you, sir?" said Francois.

"You are Francois Mayeux?" said the lieutenant.

"Yes, I am. What can I do for you?"

"It seems that a crime has been committed," the lieutenant said. "We are here to talk to your son, Pierre, about Mr. Patin."

"Pierre," said Francois in disbelief. "Are you sure you are not looking for my eldest son, Nicholas? What on earth did Pierre do?"

"We need to bring your son in for questioning. Is he here?"

"Hold on, let me see," said Francois. He closed the door and turned to go up the stairs to Pierre's bedroom.

At forty-nine years of age, Francois Mayeux had managed to ascend the social classes through a life of unexpected difficulties with no formal education. He was a self-made man and had become financially successful through fortunate mistakes. He was not the most liked man in this northwestern French province. Although not the oldest profession in the world, his line of work as a tax farmer for the Crown was just as detested by many. The French Crown divided its tax collection duties for France into provinces. Francois won the right to collect the king's taxes in the Picardy Province of the Kingdom of France by being the highest bidder at the Crown's auction. He paid a fixed annual price of 60,000 livres to the king in monthly payments of 5,000 livres. His farming contract lasted for a six-year term. Francois was now in his third contract. He had established a good relationship with the officials of the Crown and had become well established in his profession. His employees would go from house to house and business to business each month to collect the Crown's taxes. If the tax collections fell short for the month, he lost money. If his collections were over the bid price of 5,000 livres, he retained the difference.

As a tax farmer, Francois knew everyone, and just about everyone knew him. He quickly realized that trouble in his household could jeopardize his livelihood. His mind began to sort out several disturbing scenarios. He climbed the stairs and walked down the long corridor to Pierre's bedroom. He heard some rustling inside. As he opened the door, he saw Simone climbing out the window.

"Stop!" he yelled. "What are you doing here? Just you wait until I get my hands on you, you witch." He turned to his son. "I told you not to have that girl in this house. Pierre, get out of bed."

Francois was well familiar with Simone and her family. They were poor, illiterate, peasant farmers who lived in a small, three-room log cabin on Francois's farm, a five hundred-arpent tract of land he managed to acquire from the profits he squeezed out of his business through the years. Simone and her mother and father were tenant farmers, and Francois knew firsthand the hard life her family lived. He desperately desired his son not to have any contact with Simone. He knew he had to do something soon before things got out of hand. But that would have to wait for another day.

"You continue to do exactly opposite from what I command. Now, the royal guard is here to arrest you. He mentioned something about a robbery of Antoine Patin and his assistant, Joubert. What have you done?"

"Father, I cannot imagine what they would want with me. I have been here with Simone all evening," said Pierre.

"That seems to be the cause of this problem," barked Francois.

Pierre followed his father out of the bedroom in stunned disbelief. Pierre's shame and remorse for disobeying his father about Simone nearly broke through in tears. And the fright of the royal guards looking for him worked on his soul. He wondered what was going to happen. A terrifying sense of disgust rushed through his entire body, nearly paralyzing his speech and legs.

"For God's sake do not say anything to them to incriminate yourself. They plan to bring you in for questioning. I will visit you after sunrise."

Francois escorted Pierre down the stairs to the front door where the guards were waiting. "Here he is. Where are you taking him?"

"We shall take him down to the jail in Maintaney for interrogation and hold him there. You can visit in the morning," said Lieutenant Jean Claude. "Get into the carriage, Pierre."

As he watched the horses clap down the road, Francois glimpsed a faint reddish yellow glimmer peeking out over the eastern horizon. The sun was shedding over a new day, and Francois feared what the coming hours would bring.

As with all kings and emperors in Europe in the year 1720, their governments relied on taxes to survive. The Kingdom of France was no different. The taille (French pronunciation: taj) was a direct land tax on the French peasantry and non-nobles in the ancient régime of France. In 1680, the system of the Ferme Générale was established, a franchised customs and excise operation in which individuals bought the right to collect the taille on behalf of the king, through six-year adjudications (some taxes, including the aides and the gabelle, had been farmed out in this way as early as 1604). The major tax collectors in this system were known as the fermiers généraux ("farmers general," in English). The taille was only one of a number of taxes. There also existed the "taillon" (a tax for military expenditures), a national salt tax (the "gabelle"), national tariffs (the "aides") on various products, including wine, and local tariffs on specialty products (the "douane"), and taxes levied on products entering a city (the "octroi"). Finally, the church benefited from a mandatory tax or tithe called the "dime."

King Louis XIV of France created several additional tax systems, including the "capitation" (begun in 1695), which touched every person, including nobles and the clergy (although exemption could be bought for a large, one-time sum) and the "dixième" (1710 to 1717), which was a true tax on income and property value and was meant to support the military.

The dixième was restarted in 1733 and in 1749, under Louis XV, a new tax based on the dixième, the "vingtième" (or "one-twentieth"), was enacted to reduce the royal deficit, and this tax continued through the ancient régime. This tax was based solely on revenues (5 percent of net earnings from land, property, commerce, industry, and from official offices), and was meant to reach all citizens regardless of status. The tax was imposed on each household and was based on how much land the household held.

Chapter Two

By 1500, the peoples of Europe had managed to survive the Middle Ages, coming out of the darkness relatively unscathed from the Black Death. The New World had only recently been discovered. Commerce and trade had become very profitable to the Kingdoms of Europe. The major players in this new world order were the Frankish Kingdom (France), England, and Hispania (Spain). The Dutch, Portuguese and Holy Roman Empire of German Nations (Austrians) also played a part. These various players had consolidated their power under their respective monarchs and religions. Queen Isabella and King Ferdinand consolidated power in Spain under the Catholic Church and had authorized the 1492 expedition of Christopher Columbus. King Louis XI and his son, Charles VIII, ruled France with the aid of the Catholic Church. Henry VIII had not yet defied the Pope to begin the English Reformation nor had Martin Luther posted his ninety-five theses on the door of a Catholic church to begin the Protestant Reformation. The Catholic Church managed to share power with the nation states under a holy alliance through the end of the 1500s. This relative peace began to crumble in 1450 with the discovery of the printing press and was completed by the discovery of a New World and the Protestant Reformation in 1517.

The discovery of the Americas by Christopher Columbus in 1492 started the race for exploration and conquest between the major European kingdoms. And the Protestant Reformation shattered the relatively stable political peace. A previously un-known new world existed and was inhabited by the indigenous people of the Americas who did not lay claim to their land. They lived on the land by the authority of their higher power, how-ever, the kingdoms of Europe thought they held the divine right from God to take possession of these lands. Through superior military power and European diseases, their conquest began in earnest in the late 1500s and by early 1600 the whole of the Old World pursued land and wealth in the New. The formation of the modern nation states had developed to the extent that by 1699 a king's main goal was the accumulation of land and resources, both foreign and domestic, to place under his rule for the expansion of his empire.

Spain laid claim to Central and South America, Mexico, and the Caribbean. Their colony proved to be the most profitable because of the large quantities of gold and silver found in the possession of the Indians. Spanish galleons made numerous trips to Spain loaded with gold and silver coins. Because of Spain's revenue source, she sent large numbers of conquista-dors, conquered the native peoples of her colonies by the late 1600s, and established a firm stronghold in Central and South America.

French and British participation in the occupation of the Americas was neither as rapid nor as successful. Royal support was far less enthusiastic because the precious metals found by Spain never materialized in North America. The kings of France, Britain, and Spain supported their colonies in the Americas in varying degrees. France was a laggard in comparison in Spain and Britain.

In 1524, King Francois I of France financed two expedi-tions of an Italian born explorer, Giovanni Verrazzano, to the newly discovered Americas in order to find a sea route to China. With the ships, *La Dauphine, Delfina, Normanda, Santa Maria* and *Vittoria,* he and his brother, Girolamo, sailed up the east coast of North America to Terra Nova (New Land). John Cabot had already claimed the island of Newfoundland for England.

Verrazzano named the region he explored, an area from the Gulf of Mexico to British Newfoundland, Francesca, in honor of the French king. Girolamo, a cartographer, labeled it *Nova Gallia* (Nouvelle France) on his map.

During the years 1534 to 1536, the French explorer Jacques Cartier made several expeditions to Nouvelle France on behalf of King Francois I. When Cartier arrived to find an uncharted gulf on the American coast on the feast day of St. Lawrence, he named it the Gulf of St. Lawrence and the river connected to it, the St. Laurent. The Iroquois were the Native Americans who inhabited the region. He sailed up-river and reached the Iroquoian capital of Stadacona, a name derived from the Iroquois word "kanata," or village. In 1541, Cartier founded Charlesbourg–Royal on the St. Laurent River, the first French settlement in the New World. The French abandoned it two years later because of constant attacks by the Indians. Several attempts by the French at founding a permanent settlement during this period failed yet the districts of Canada, Hudson Bay and Acadia became the territory of Nouvelle France.

Tadoussac, Quebec, Canada was finally permanently settled by the French in 1599 as a fur trading post at the mouth of the Saguenay River, at its confluence with the St. Laurent. Port-Royal, Acadia was settled by the French in 1605 on the coast. Port-Royal served as the capital of Acadia until its destruction by British forces in 1613, so France relocated the settlement and capital to the other side of the peninsula of Acadia. The relocated settlement kept the name Port-Royal and served as the capital of French Acadia for one hundred years, the majority of the 17th century. By comparison, Jamestown was founded by the British in 1607 in New England, making it the first permanent British colony in the New World.

Francois Mayeux was born in Maintenay, France in 1670 and escaped poverty by migrating to Paris in his teens. He met and married his wife, Marie Breslin in 1690. Marie was from a court official's family in Paris. They met while Francois was flirting with the idea of joining a Franciscan monastery there. The allures of the present world overpowered his godly pursuits and he soon forgot his desire for preparing his soul for the afterlife. Marie Breslin became his savior. Their first child, Nicholas, was born in Paris in 1692 and their second, Emily, was born in 1695. Their third child, Pierre Mayeux, was born in Maintenay on August 26, 1699, a turbulent time in French history, and for that matter, a turbulent time in world politics.

Francois groomed Pierre into an honest and fine young man, although he could not remove a wild streak of indifference about him. Pierre had a loving and affectionate side to his disposition, though he had not yet fully discovered it. Francois sought to give all his children advantages he never had. He employed a governess for Pierre when the boy was only four years old. She was from Paris and taught Pierre the Latin and English languages while she schooled him in French. She was well versed in reading, writing, and arithmetic. Once her charge reached eleven years old, she was dismissed and sought new employment.

Unlike his governess, who had lived within the Mayeux household, Pierre's tutor came to the house five days a week and taught him music and finance. With his formal education nearly complete, Pierre had been working in his father's tax farm for the last year and was exceeding his father's expectations. Pierre had been secretly seeking Simone's affections for the last six months, a lesson not taught to him by his governess or his tutor. He was learning this lesson by trial and error. His supposed secret had not escaped the experienced and watchful eye of Francois, however. Francois and Marie, Pierre's mother, did not approve of the relationship. They wanted Pierre to follow in the footsteps of his sister, Emily, and attend the Sorbonne in Paris. But Pierre found Simone seductively attractive and this distraction awakened newly discovered desires in the confused nineteen year old. He didn't know whether he was madly in love with her or whether she was just filling an empty space in his heart.

Emily had married and moved out of the Mayeux household about two years before. She and her husband lived in Paris. Nicholas, Francois's eldest son, had a pretended air of sophistication about him. Firstborns are like that. Francois had managed to corral Pierre much better than Nicholas, who drank too much and was a womanizer. Nicholas's illegitimate child, now five years old, brought much disgrace to Francois and Marie, but they loved the child just the same. The estranged mother always fermented Francois' anger. She lived with another man who was the father of her second child, and she often used the grandchild as a weapon against Francois. He had decided that he and the mother would never get along. Francois allowed Nicholas to work for the tax farm too, but Nicholas never managed a steady work week.

After the guards left with Pierre, François could not go back to sleep. The events of that morning had upset him and stirred his emotions. Sleep had become impossible. His mind rehearsed the events of the morning and possible consequences. He paced the kitchen floor and stoked the hearth fire in the kitchen, contemplating his next move. By that time, Marie was dressed and had come downstairs. The creaking stairs returned Francois' thoughts to reality.

"What is going on?" asked Marie. "With all the commotion, I could not get the story from you."

"It seems that damned Antoine Patin is at it again," said Francois. "This time he has carried it a little too far. He has accused Pierre of robbing him last night, in the early evening of yesterday, I think. He claims he has a witness, his assistant, Joubert. The royal guard has taken Pierre into custody."

"I can't believe that of Pierre," said Marie in a panic. "He would never do such a thing." She began to sob.

"I don't believe he could do such a thing, either," Francois replied. "I am going to get to the bottom of this. You know why he is up to no good—that scoundrel Antoine Patin has always wanted my tax farm. His tax farm is not making any livre in the small province he has."

"Don't do anything drastic," said Marie. "We don't need you in jail too."

"I will visit Pierre this morning and get the whole story from him," said Francois.

Marie rustled the coals in the hearth and put on a pot of water to make coffee. She decided the servant would cook a light breakfast. Marie was an elegant lady who supervised a staff of only two employees: Henrietta, who cooked and cleaned, and Joseph, who took care of the animals, the grounds, barn, and carriage house. She managed to keep the house always running smoothly. With only Pierre left at the house, life was not as hectic as her earlier years.

Nicholas would come and go, staying over for a few nights and disappearing again. Marie spent most of her days taking care of Pierre and Francois. She had developed a close relationship with Pierre and was greatly distressed at the thought that he was now sitting in a jail cell all alone.

"Here's your breakfast," said Lieutenant Jean Claude. "Hurry up and eat. You are going to Amiens."

"Bread and water," said Pierre. "That's surely not fit for a king."

"Kings have no place where you are going," said Lieutenant Jean Claude. Pierre hurriedly ate as he didn't know when he would have another chance for food.

Francois arrived on horseback at the small jail, eager to check on his son. The jail was a two-room building, a front office, and a cell. It never had that much business. It was located in the center of Maintenay not far from the Catholic church of the parish, which was the lowest level of administrative division in the Kingdom of France. When a hamlet became large enough to justify a church, it became a village. The church was always the focal point of any village or town. The priest of the church normally came from the nobility. They recorded baptisms, marriages, and burials as well as the regular duties of Mass and confession. The parish church often owned outlying buildings and properties, including farmland. This local church was no different. Father Hebert received most of his income from the land.

The village of Maintenay had only about fifty homes, made of red clay bricks and wooden beams. Surrounding the village were vast areas of farmland, of which Francois owned his track. The village contained several small office buildings and many shops, including a boucherie that provided fresh meats. The local farmers at the farmers' market provided fresh vegetables. The sole bakery supplied fresh bread. Maintenay was a cozy little village.

"I am here to see my son, Pierre," said Francois as he entered the jailhouse. Lieutenant Jean Claude greeted him as he walked in.

"Sorry sir, you will not be able to visit Pierre this morning. We are taking him to Amiens this minute to face his accusers."

Francois did not argue. He immediately realized the gravity of the situation. At that moment, a large stagecoach pulled up at the front of the jail. Francois noticed the driver was armed with a musket.

"Father," exclaimed Pierre, as he was lead out of the backroom cell in handcuffs. "Please, help me."

"I will take care of it, Pierre. I will talk to my advocate in Amiens as soon as possible and get you out."

The lieutenant rushed Pierre into the waiting stagecoach and the driver yelled at the two horses with a flip of the reins. The stagecoach sped off, heading south to Amiens on the King's Highway. The city of Amiens was the provincial capitol of Picardy Province. It laid some thirty leagues south of Maintenay, a half-day journey by horseback. Amiens was about forty leagues north of Paris, the capitol of the Kingdom of France.

Francois rode straight to his office in the village of Maintenay. As he walked in, he noticed Nicholas standing in the front office, flirting with a female clerk. "I am afraid I have some bad news," Francois said. "Your brother has been arrested."

"Imagine that, I thought I was the black sheep in this family. What did he do?" asked Nicholas.

"Antoine Patin swore out an affidavit that Pierre robbed him."

"That dirty bastard," said Nicholas. "I should take a bayonet to him. He knows our monopoly near the coast is much more profitable than his. Those sea merchants sure bring in the livre. What will we do?"

"You will do nothing," said Francois. "I will take Henri with me to Amiens. We will bring in the tax receipts a week earlier than expected. Where is Henri?"

"Here, in the back," hollered Henri.

Henri was the office manager, and like Francois, was a part of the Third Estate and a relatively wealthy member of the bourgeoisie. His white hair showed his age. He had worked with Francois for some fifteen years, since the beginning of his tax farm business, and Henri had always been a loyal employee. They had met while Francois was in Paris discovering himself in his youth. Henri had been Francois's best man at his wedding and had been his confidant ever since. Like most bourgeoisie who made their fortunes in a trade or business, the two men had ploughed their money into home and farmland purchases and were able to educate their children, who in turn went into professions of their own.

"Henri, we need to leave for Amiens early in the morning," said Francois. "Pierre has been arrested and has been taken there. Gather the receipts collected so for this month. Go home and pack, and meet me at my house at daybreak. We will be gone for a few days so pack accordingly. Nicholas, you shall be in charge in my absence."

Upon arrival in Amiens, Pierre was thrown into a dark and grimy jail cell. The only light came from a small window down the long stone corridor with cells on either side, all of which were filled with prisoners. Most were screaming, hollering, or moaning because of their dire circumstances. The whole building was dark and damp and smelled of a rotting dung heap. It was a living hell to Pierre.

Was incarceration his final reward for his deliberate indifference towards his heretofore-good life in Maintenay? A crisis of conscience ensued. Pierre questioned his faith in God, or rather, the faith he thought he had. He wondered whether the Catholic rituals that had been hammered into his head from childhood still meant anything to his suffering soul. Was this a punishment for not strictly following his Catholic faith and the commands of his father? Were his sexual frolics with Simone the cause?

"Why am I here?" he thought aloud. He was in a state of absolute distress.

Closing his eyes, he saw a countenance of death and sunk to the gates of Hell. It was the lowest point of his life. He questioned his reason for living. Depression overcame him, and he flirted with thoughts of suicide. He rehearsed in his mind how much he loved Simone and how much his father and mother disagreed with his relationship with her. He sobbed when he thought about the pain he was causing his loving mother who was always a source of encouragement when he cut his knee or made failing grades as a child. She was such a loving, caring, and compassionate person compared to his father who always seemed cold and distant. He began to cry thinking about the criminal charges pending against him. His lack of freedom behind bars compounded his misery. The distress of being locked up in such horrible conditions immediately began to take its toll. His mind wandered with an acute awareness. Pierre had never experienced a consciousness of such debilitating distress. This discernment of mental pain caused his life to rush before him. Freedom became a cherished commodity in his captivity. He felt utterly helpless and in total agony. He was spiritually bankrupt and he knew it. He mourned under the burden of not knowing his fate and future.

He got down on his knees, on the hard damp floor of his cell, and prayed out loud to God. "Lord, please forgive me for my sins, my sex with Simone outside of marriage, my not following the sacraments of my Catholic faith, my lack of repentance with a contrite heart, and my disdain for my father. Please forgive me and give me strength to make it through this ordeal. I will accept your commands. I surrender to you. Whatever your will, Lord, I will accept."

"Shut up your crying and moaning," said a fellow prisoner in the next cell. "You will never get out of here."

Pierre then resigned himself and swore to God that if he were to get out of prison, he would attempt to lead a godly life. He decided that he would marry Simone, move out of his father's house and into a place of his own. He would stay with his father's business until one day he could inherit it and continue it as a success to make his father proud.

"I have been falsely accused," Pierre shouted to his fellow prisoners, grasping the iron bars of his cell and shaking them violently. "And I will get out of here."

The royal families throughout Europe ruled by divine right as if it were a directive from God. These royal dynasties often intermarried within and between dynasties. Kings from the House of Bourbon ruled France. The Holy Roman Empire, consisting of the kingdoms of Germany and Italy (but never the city of Rome), was ruled by the House of Habsburgs (also referred to as the House of Austria). The House was originally from Switzerland and ruled from Austria but eventually brought all of central Europe under its control, including Spain. On April 21, 1521, Holy Roman Emperor Charles V split the dynasty into two branches. He became King of Spain assuming a new name, Charles I, under the Spanish Habsburgs and his brother, Ferdinand I, retained the Austrian lands. The Austrian Habsburgs retained the title of Holy Roman Emperor.

The first Bourbon King in France was Henry IV, in 1589. Although baptized a Catholic, Henry was raised a Protestant, but he eventually proclaimed Catholicism as the official religion of his empire, in 1598. Religious tension had ebbed and flowed in France since the beginning of the Protestant Reformation. The Huguenots, the French Protestants (also called Calvinists), were allowed freedom of worship, though. Henry IV's proclamation of Catholicism as the official French religion allowed Protestants some freedoms and temporarily stopped the religious strife taking place in France at the time. Henry IV's first marriage produced no heirs. His second marriage to Marie de Medici produced a son, Louis XIII born on September 27, 1601. His other children included Elisabeth, who would become Queen of Spain, and Henriette Marie, the eventual Queen of England, Ireland, and Scotland.

French nobleman Pierre Dugua was granted the exclusive right to establish a settlement on the peninsula of Acadia in June 1604 under the authority of Henry IV. Pierre Dugua and Samuel de Champlain founded Port-Royal, the capital of Acadia, in 1605 and it became the first permanent French settlement in the New World. (Two years later, the English made their first permanent settlement in Jamestown.) Champlain founded Quebec City on July 3, 1608 at the site of the then abandoned Indian settlement of Stadacona. Champlain served as its administrator for the rest of his life. He made an alliance with the Hurons and fought the Iroquois who became mortal enemies of New France. Champlain served as the first commandant general of New France from 1627 through 1635. Henry IV was assassinated by a fanatical Catholic on May 14, 1610 in Paris.

Henry IV's son, Louis XIII, at only nine years of age, rose to the throne. Because he was too young to rule, his mother, Marie de Medici, served as regent until he became of age at thirteen. His mother advanced a pro-Spanish foreign policy, as she was a descendant of the Habsburg dynasty, the royal family of Spain and The Holy Roman Empire. In November 1615, Marie arranged Louis XIII's marriage to Anne of Austria, the daughter of King Philip III of Spain, a tradition of cementing military and political alliances between the Catholic powers of France and Spain. Louis XIII and Anne of Austria were married on November 24, 1615. After twenty-three years of marriage and four misconceptions, they finally had a son, Louis XIV, born on September 5, 1638. Their second child was Philippe I, Duke of

Orleans. After his coronation on October 17, 1610, Louis XIII, along with his chief minister, Cardinal Richelieu, a nobleman and bishop in the Catholic church, took interest in organizing and developing the colony of New France in the New World, efforts that had been largely abandoned due to the failure of Charlesbourg-Royal on the St. Laurent River some seventy-five years earlier. Nouvelle France began to grow with new emigrant arrivals financed by French nobles seeking financial gain. Louis XIII died on May 14, 1643 at the age of forty-two.

Chapter Three

In 1627, Cardinal Richelieu, King Louis XIII's chief minister, introduced the seigneurial system in New France. Cardinal Richelieu formed the Company of One Hundred Associates to invest in New France, promising land grants to new settlers. Only Roman Catholics were allowed to go to New France. Protestants were forbidden land grants. Under this system, the land along the St. Laurent was arranged in long narrow strips called seigneuries with each lot usually having river frontage. The king owned all of the land but a nobleman, called a seigneur, managed it. By this time, the feudal system in France was disappearing and the estate classes began. The seigneurs in New France were not always noblemen but included military officers and the clergy. The seigneur divided the land further among the habitants. The habitants paid taxes to the seigneur and had to do work for him for a number of days per year. They cleared the land, built houses, and farmed the land but had more freedom than the peasants of the mother country. In fact, they refused to be called peasants.

The King of France, through divine right, ruled the Kingdom of France and New France with the explicit support of the Catholic Church. Under the king, the rest of French society divided itself into three groups of estates. The First Estate was the clergy of the Catholic Church, the official religion of France. The church owned nearly a tenth of all land in France, including numerous churches and outbuildings. Villages, towns, and cities were always organized around a church and the priests and bishops held great authority. The church hierarchy mostly came from the nobility. The church parishes formed the backbone of the political makeup of the provinces. King Louis XIV boasted of ruling over his "realm of one hundred thousand steeples."

The Second Estate was the nobility, people born into families descending from the various kings. They often held offices in the king's court, the judicial system, and other governmental offices. Often, persons of means purchased the right of nobility and thus a position in government.

The remainder of the French population, roughly 98 percent, was from the Third Estate. They were usually illiterate peasant farmers, unable to read or write, working for the seigneur, the landlords. However, a small portion belonged to the bourgeoisie.

Ville-Marie, later called Montreal, was founded in 1642, a year before Louis XIV began his reign as a boy king, when his father, Louis XIII, died. This fort was west of Quebec City on the St. Laurent. Throughout this period, the French were constantly at war with the Indians and the English. The French and Iroquois Wars began in 1642. The year 1649 saw the beginning of the total elimination of the Huron Indian nation by the Iroquois. The population of the French colony and the expansion of its borders for the French Crown grew very slowly.

Francois arose early, long before sunrise. He finished packing his things in a couple of leather bags and placed them by the front door. He was in the kitchen with Henrietta when Marie came down.

"Good morning, Henrietta," said Marie in a sullen voice.

"Good morning."

"Can you prepare Francois a large breakfast?" asked Marie. "He is going away for a few days and we want to send him off with a full stomach. Please pack him a lunch, too."

"Yes, Madame, I'll cook ham, eggs, and biscuits. I wish Pierre were here to enjoy them," said Henrietta. As she threw a couple of pieces of wood on the open fire of the fireplace, she realized she may have spoken out of turn.

"So do I," said Marie as she retired to the parlor to join Francois. "I think I will pen a letter to Pierre."

"That is a great idea. I am sure Pierre would appreciate hearing some encouraging words from you," he replied.

Marie opened her desk drawer, took out a parchment, and began writing with pen and ink, her words illuminated by candlelight.

Dear Pierre, my beloved son,

We miss you so much here at home. I know in my heart that you did not and could not have done those bad things they allege. I know your father will secure your release and you will be back with us in no time. Keep your faith in God, be strong, and I will see you soon.

Your Loving Mother

Marie folded the parchment, sealed it with wax and her seal, and handed it to Francois, who placed it in his coat pocket.

"I will give it to him as soon as I see him today," Francois said. "Don't worry, everything will be well."

"I am so afraid for him," said Marie. "You must bring him home."

After breakfast, Marie heard a horse gallop up to the house. Henri arrived right on time, just as the sun began to peek over the horizon. Francois hurriedly made his way to the carriage porch. The coach with two horses was waiting.

"Good morning, Henri," said Francois. "Joseph rigged my covered carriage in case of bad weather. Joseph, take Henri's horse to the carriage house for boarding. Did you arrange for a coachman?"

"Yes, sir," said Joseph. "I spoke with Landis, your usual driver, yesterday. I don't know where he could be."

Joseph led Henri's horse to the carriage house as Landis came barreling in on his horse. Landis went immediately to the carriage house, tied up his horse, and met Francois and Henri at the carriage porch at the front of the house.

"Good morning, sir, sorry I am late," said Landis.

"I see you brought your musket with bayonet," said Henri.

"Yes, sir, you never know who you might meet on the King's Highway. It's best to be prepared."

"Let us be on our way. Landis, help Joseph secure the baggage. Did you bring your pistol, Henri?" asked Francois.

"Yes, and I placed the tax receipts inside the trap door in the floor of the carriage," said Henri. "They are not near the usual amount since we are going so early this month. My pistol is in there, too."

After everything was stowed away and Francois and Henri boarded the carriage, Landis cracked the reins, and they were off. Marie waved from the porch as the coach sped down the dirt road towards Amiens. The three had made this same trip on numerous occasions, though they journeyed together only in exceptional occasions, like this one. This time, Pierre was at the heart of the trip.

Their journey to Amiens took most of the day. They arrived in Amiens in early evening, just before dark. The city was bustling with people making their way between work and home, stopping at the boucherie and bakery for supplies to prepare for supper. Francois ordered Landis to head straight to the Royal Bank so he could turn in the tax receipts, knowing that holding them overnight would only create additional problems. The carriage, under Landis' control, came to a raging stop in front of the bank just before closing time. Francois decided to go into the bank without Landis or Henri.

"Good evening," he said to the clerk sitting behind the desk as he quickly walked through the stately entrance. "Is Mr. Arnaud still in?"

"You may catch him if you hurry, Mr. Mayeux. I don't think he left for the evening," said the clerk.

"Francois, you are here early this month," said Arnaud as Francois walked into his office. "I was just leaving for the day."

"Yes, for a reason. My son, Pierre, has been arrested and is in the custody of the Crown, so I had to come early. I must get him out tomorrow," Francois explained with a heavy heart. "That damned Antione Patin accused him of robbery."

"I heard about the crime just today from another tax collector. He said that the robbery occurred in Antoine Patin's section of Picardy Province. Is it true?" asked Arnaud.

"Of course not," said Francois. "Antoine is up to his old tricks, but this time he has carried it a little too far."

"You know we do not need any trouble in the Northern provinces. The financial condition of France is in dire straits. The stock price for the Mississippi Company has risen to 14,500 livres a share. You know, you should sell the shares you have been accumulating. Rumor has it that John Law and the Regent, Philippe II, the Duke of Orleans, plan to devalue the stock. I sold my stock two days ago and made a handsome profit. I knew this frenzy in the stock market would not last. I only wish our child king would hurry and become of age to get rid of that scoundrel, John Law," said Arnaud.

He took a look at the tax receipts Francois had brought in.

"Your receipts look all in order, but it is not as much as last month. Oh, I forgot, you are here early this month. Your coastal district in Picardy has done well for you over the years. You know, it would be a shame that you lose it. Be sure to straighten out this mess with Pierre," said Arnaud.

"I shall, but I may need your help if things become difficult" said Francois with a renewed sense of urgency. "You have always been such a loyal friend. I will try my damnedest to keep you out of this. I am on my way to see Pierre now. I will see you next month, and I will take your advice on the stock sale."

Francois made his way to the front entrance. The clerk had to let him out, as the doors had already been locked for the evening. Henri and Landis were waiting patiently in the carriage.

"Landis, take us to the jail house. I think it is on Rue Louis XIV, a few blocks pass the church and to the right. Hurry, it's getting dark."

Landis made his way through the streets of the city, barely avoiding the pedestrians. The only light in the streets was from the candlelight cascading from the windows of houses and businesses.

He drove up to an old stone building with a placard hanging over the front door. It was the jailhouse. Candles burned inside the window.

"Must still be open," said Landis to Francois as Francois hurriedly exited the carriage and raced to the entrance. He bolted through the front door with a mission.

"I am here to see Pierre Mayeux," he said to the guard sitting behind the desk.

"Sorry, sir, you will have to return tomorrow," said the guard.

"But I have not spoken with my son since he was arrested. I demand to see him," said Francois with a raised voice.

"The prisoners are all fed and locked down for the night. You will have to come back in the morning—unless you want to spend the night here," said the guard, getting angry.

"Father, is that you? Get me out of here!" hollered Pierre from somewhere deep within the hollow cavern.

The guard rose from his chair, grabbed Francois by the arm, and immediately escorted him to the front door.

"You need to leave now before you excite all the prisoners," ordered the guard as he opened the door and forced Francois into the street. Landis and Henri were there waiting.

"To the Boor's Nest Inn," ordered Francois to Landis as he entered the coach in disgust. "I could not see him tonight. I will visit the first thing in the morning and then make a visit to our advocate for legal advice."

"Pierre must be in more serious trouble than we thought," said Henri.

Night had fallen over the city of Amiens. The only light was from the full moon. Landis enjoyed the cool spring evening air as he drove the carriage to the inn. The city gleamed with a surreal enchantment. Landis thought it looked a bit like his hometown in the countryside, aglow by the light of a thousand lightning bugs.

"Karlis's Livery is the stable I normally use," Francois barked to Landis. "Drive there, but first help Henri and me with the luggage. Meet us here after you board the horses." Francois and Henri exited the carriage in front of the Boor's Nest Inn.

Upon arrival at the livery, Landis was greeted by the stable hand that then led the carriage and horses into the huge building. A number of horses were in the stables already and several carriages were parked in a row in one corner of the building. Breastplates, harnesses, bridles, and saddles lined another wall. A stable boy was feeding the horses hay.

"That will be ten livres per night," said the stable boy.

"My God, the price has gone up. But I have none. Put it on the account for Francois Mayeux. We will return in the morning. Make sure to feed and water the horses. They have been riding all day," said Landis.

He walked over to the Boor's Nest, which was only a block away from the livery. Henri and Francois were in their rooms already. Landis checked with the desk clerk and was directed to his room. He knocked on the door of Francois's room.

"Come in."

"The horses are boarded, sir. Is there anything else?"

"Please go down to the desk and get a lettersheet and sealing wax. I think I will write a letter to Marie," said Francois. "Can you drop it at the Royal Postal Service in the morning? I should inquire about getting a part of that postal monopoly," Francois murmured.

When Landis returned with the lettersheet and wax, he went to bed, exhausted from driving the carriage all day. Francois sat at the small table in his room and began to write by the light of a small candle, using the quill pen from the ink well provided by the inn.

Monday, April 15, 1720
Dear Marie,

Our carriage ride to Amiens was uneventful. We are here safe at the Boor's Nest Inn. I was unable to see Pierre today, but I will visit him the first thing in the morning. I will give him your love and best wishes. We may be here for a few more days, but please do not worry. When we return home, I shall have our beloved Pierre.

Your Loving Husband, Francois

Francois folded the lettersheet and wrote *Marie Mayeux* and *Maintenay Post* on the front. He melted the sealing wax by the flame of the candle. A few drops fell on the folded letter. As the wax was drying, he thought of Pierre in prison and wondered if he would accomplish his task and get him out. He applied his signet ring to the soft wax, blew out his candle, and climbed into bed. He was exhausted from the journey and went immediately to sleep.

John Law was born into a family of bankers and goldsmiths in Scotland. He was well versed in the laws of finance and commerce. Upon his father's death, he squandered his inheritance gambling throughout Europe. People described him as tall, handsome, and vain. His passion for women and gambling led him to France in 1714 to renew his acquaintance with Philippe II, Duke of Orleans. When the duke became Regent of France, Law realized the opportunity that faced him. Law approached the regent with the idea of forming a national public bank. When the Parlement de Paris objected to the idea, the regent gave him a private charter and Law began the Bank Generale (royal bank) by publicly issuing twelve hundred shares at a price of five thousand livres each. Law and the regent each bought a quarter of the shares. The private bank issued paper notes payable in silver coins on demand. Getting the notes to circulate and not returned for redemption became a huge problem. The regent and several noblemen made large deposits in an attempt to keep the notes in circulation. A royal decree on October 17, 1716 required the tax collectors to redeem the banknotes on demand with the result of making the notes legal tender for taxes. The decentralized nature of tax collection with France's tax farms helped the financial endeavor take root. Tax collectors were required to keep accounts and turn in receipts in banknotes.

The regent was impressed with this new concept of paper money. The regent, upon Law's suggestion, nationalized the bank in December 1718 and bought out all existing shareholders. John Law, with the backing of Regent Philippe II and on behalf of the king, would manage the royal bank. All profits would be turned over to the royal treasury. Initial investors made huge returns from the stock buyback, and it proved to the gullible public the gains one could make by investing in any company started by John Law.

Chapter Four

"**P**lease tell my traveling companions, Henri and Landis, when they get up, that I have gone to the café next door," said Francois to the desk clerk of the inn the next morning. As Francois stepped out the front door, he came upon a young lad selling newsletters. "Is that the *La Gazette de France*? Give me a copy," said Francois.

"That will be one livre, sir," said the boy.

Francois entered the café. He commanded a seat by the window, as the place was not yet crowded this early in the morning. "I'll have chicory coffee and beignets," he told the waiter as he settled in to read the news of the day.

Most of the articles were about New France and about the exploits of the Mississippi Company in the Louisiana colony. He noticed a small story in the bottom corner about the national debt. His main concern was whether Pierre's arrest had made the newsletter. It would not be good for his business. He searched and searched again, but luckily, he did not find a story about the arrest.

"The clerk told us we would find you here," said Henri, interrupting Francois's thoughts. Henri and Landis took a seat at the table and each ordered breakfast.

"I think I will pay a visit to my advocate, Avery Legard, this morning before we visit Pierre, instead of going straight to the jail," said Francois.

"That may be a good idea," said Henri. "He may suggest a route to secure Pierre's release. Any good news for Pierre is bound to lift his spirits."

"Ah, here's our breakfast," said Landis. The smell of bacon had followed the server from the kitchen. Landis was more interested in the plate she placed in front of him than the delightful looking young brunette.

"Well, this is the plan. Landis will get the carriage and pick us up at the inn. Henri and I shall pay a visit to Mr. Legard while Landis drops my letter to Marie at the Royal Post. Then we shall visit Pierre," said Francois. "Let's eat."

"Only one problem," said Landis. "I will need ten livres in order to retrieve the carriage from the stable and extra livre to pay the postal company."

"Ten livres per day? That is highway robbery," said Henri.

"*Oui, les temps changent,*" agreed Francois. "The price of everything seems to be steadily going up."

After breakfast, Francois and Henri left for the advocate's office with Landis in the coachman's seat. There, they found a clerk attending to paperwork at his desk.

"Bonjuor, monsieur. Is Mr. Avery Legard in? Can you tell him Francois Mayeux is here to see him?"

"I will check. Please have a seat," said the clerk, directing Francois and Henri to two old chairs in the lobby.

Francois had been to his advocate's office on numerous occasions. Mr. Legard handled all of his legal problems and land transactions. Henri used his services as well.

"Francois and Henri, good to see you. To what do I owe this pleasure?" asked Mr. Legard as he directed Francois and Henri into his office. "Please have a seat."

"Let me be direct, Avery," said Francois. "My son, Pierre, was arrested in Maintenay for the robbery of Antoine Patin. He was transported here to Amiens for trial and is being held by the royal guard. We must get him released. What can we do?"

"I did notice a Mayeux on the criminal docket," said Avery, "but I did not know it was your son."

"How do these criminal proceedings work?" asked Francois.

"Our inquisitorial system is usually based on quick and quasi secret judicial proceedings. It can be arbitrary and sometimes repressive. Good for us, Magistrate Reynard came up from the social classes. He is not of nobility. He mostly follows royal enactments, church law, and our local customs but he is especially keen on exemptions or privileges extended from the Parlement de Paris, the judicial branch of the King's Court, or, more importantly, from the regent. There is a royal ordinance on criminal law. However, it is very strict. Punishments can sometimes be severe. The Parlement de Paris does like to pretend at its independence by protesting the excesses of royal decrees at times, and will on occasion extend leniency for us locals, but I think your best chance is with the regent," said Avery.

"When will the trial be held?" asked Francois.

"I do not know. However, it will be soon. I will have to inquire," said Avery. "I do have a contact in the royal court. The regent is still running the show as if he is king, and as you know, he is in cahoots with John Law and that bunch. My contact's name is Guillaume Dubois, the regent's chief minister. You will need to go to Paris and beg for a plea bargain. I will prepare for you a letter of introduction," said Avery.

"Good. We shall leave for Paris as soon as we visit Pierre," said Francois. "We will stop by here before we leave to see if you can get the court date, and we will pick up the letter of introduction. I owe you so much for this, Avery."

Francois and Henri made for the exit. Landis was waiting outside at the helm of the carriage, gawking at the pretty girls passing by.

"To the jailhouse," said Francois to Landis as he and Henri entered the carriage. Francois felt an emotional relief with the possibility of Pierre's freedom, but the reality was that his freedom was not certain yet.

Upon arrival at the jailhouse, Francois decided Henri and Landis would check out of the inn and deposit the letter to Marie at the post. He would visit Pierre alone.

"I am here to see my son, Pierre Mayeux," said Francois to the guard sitting at the front desk. The guard, an older gentleman with gray hair, was a different guard from the night before. Francois's politeness revealed this guard's temperament to be more pleasing and cooperative than the night watch guard.

"Sign your name and put the date here," said the old guard. "And follow me."

Francois was nervous with anticipation. He had come this far, and his only hope was that fate would intervene. Surely nothing more sinister could happen to Pierre. A miracle was needed. He was glad that he was going to finally be able to speak with his son. He had never been in the bowels of a prison before. It was dark, rank, and emitting foul odors. The conditions made him feel sorry for Pierre.

"Have a seat in this room, and I will get your son," said the old guard as he motioned to a small room with a tiny table and two chairs. The only light poured in through a small window with iron bars.

In only a short time, Francois heard the clinking of chains and then Pierre appeared at the door with the old guard following close behind. Francois was astounded. Pierre's clothing was dirty, wet, and tattered. His hair was soiled and he had gone unshaven for some days now. Pierre's legs and hands were chained together. He did manage a smile when he saw his father.

"Have a seat," ordered the guard to Pierre. "We only allow five minutes per visit, but I will give you a little more time, Mr. Mayeux. I like you. I will be back when your time is up."

Francois did not know where to start.

"Looks like it's hell in here. How have you been getting along?" asked Francois.

"Father, I so desperately want to get out of here. I don't know how much more I can stand."

"Have you made any statements to anyone about the crime for which you are charged?" asked Francois.

"No, I have not said anything to anyone. What have you heard?"

"They say you robbed Antoine Patin, and he has a witness, but I have not seen the sworn affidavit. Did you do it?" asked Francois.

"Father, I must confess. Simone and I had been drinking, and she was complaining about her family not having enough food. We were walking back to our house from her house, and I noticed a buggy coming down the road. It was dark. She decided to rob them. I tried to talk her out of it, but it all happened so quickly. She grabbed my pistol, stopped the buggy, and demanded money. Of all the people it could have been, it was Antoine Patin and his driver. He threw down a bag. Simone grabbed it and we ran off. He must have recognized me."

"For God's sake, Pierre, I have told you that you need to stay away from that girl. She is trouble and will only bring you heartache and despair."

"But father, I love her. I have decided to marry her if I get out of here alive."

"Pierre, since your birth, I have wanted nothing but the best for you. You excelled in your education and have been doing so well with the business, but you insist on attaching yourself to that girl. Look where it has gotten you. You are only twenty years old. You know nothing of this world. Your mother has sheltered you. Your tutors have taught you only book sense."

Francois paused for a moment and realized now was not the time for lecturing. He also immediately became conscious that he had not been personally involved in Pierre's personal life and spiritual fortitude as he should have been throughout Pierre's boyhood. But Pierre's physical life was now at stake.

"Here's a letter from your mother. Read it later. I have spoken to Avery, my advocate. He has a contact in Paris that may be of some help. Henri and I are off to Paris at this very moment. We will be back for your trial, if they haven't hanged you first, and hopefully with some good news."

"Father, there is one other thing. Along with the tax collections Simone received as booty, the bag contained Antoine's financial records. He is keeping two sets of books, one with the actual tax receipts and another that he reports to the Crown. Simone has them both."

Francois gazed at Pierre with amazement.

As Francois struggled to show some empathy for his son and express the love he felt for him, the old guard returned and began to slowly unlock the door to the tiny visiting room. Pierre detected an unexpected affection from his father and wanted to say that he loved him but the indifference became deliberate. He could not muster the words because of the embarrassment of never having said them before.

"Your time is up," said the old guard. "Hope you had a good visit."

"Tell Henri hello, and tell mother I love her," said Pierre as the old guard led him back to his cell. "Please, father, get me out of here."

French King Louis XIV, also known as the Sun King, rose to the throne at four years of age when his father, Louis XIII died in 1643. Louis XIV was a product of noteworthy European ruling houses. His paternal grandparents were Henry IV and Marie de' Medici of the Bourbon dynasty. Both his maternal grandparents were Habsburgs—Philip III of Spain and Margaret of Austria. His reign, from 1643 to his death in 1715, lasted seventy-two years, three months, and eighteen days, and is the longest documented reign of any European monarch. Louis XIV began personally governing France in 1661 at the age of twenty-two after the death of his prime minister, the acting regent. Louis created a centralized state government from his capital. He sought to eliminate the remnants of the feudal system, which still existed in parts of France. He tried to reduce the national debt through more efficient taxation. The principal taxes included the customs duties, a tax on salt, and a tax on land. He encouraged the development of the new colony of Canada in the New World. He explored the Mississippi River and began the colonization of the Louisiana colony. He strengthened France's control over the West Indies and trade from the islands flourished. His edict regarding slavery in the islands under French control in the Caribbean was promulgated in 1685. The Code Noir was recorded at the Superior Council of Saint-Domingue on May 6, 1687.

For much of Louis XIV's reign, France stood as the leading European power, engaging in three major wars, including the War of the Spanish Succession and two minor conflicts. Through four main building campaigns, Louis converted a hunting lodge built by Louis XIII into the grand Palace of Versailles. Louis officially moved the royal court to Versailles on May 6, 1682. Louis also achieved increased control over the French aristocracy. Pensions and privileges necessary to live in a style appropriate to their rank were only possible by waiting constantly on Louis. He compelled and seduced the old military aristocracy, the nobility, the cardinals and clergy into becoming his ceremonial courtiers at Versailles. They depended on him for their every need. Brought up to respect Catholicism, Louis was a pious and devout king. Seeing himself as the protector of the French Church, he made his devotions every day, wherever he was, following regularly the liturgical calendar. Louis saw the persistence of Protestantism as a disgrace.

Responding to petitions of his subjects, Louis initially excluded Protestants from office, closed churches, banned Protestant outdoor preachers, and prohibited domestic Protestant migration. He also disallowed Protestant-Catholic intermarriages and rewarded converts to Catholicism. His Edict of Fontainebleau exiled pastors, demolished churches, instituted forced baptisms, and banned Protestant groups. Because of this persecution, about two hundred thousand Huguenots (roughly 27 percent of the Protestant population, or 1 percent of the French population) fled France, taking with them their skills and resources.

In 1663, King Louis XIV cancelled the contract of the Company of the One Hundred Associates, took over the administration of New France, and established a royal government in the New World. Responsibilities for finance, justice, and the police went to the intendant, a new position in the French government. The intendant managed the budget, set prices, organized the census, and chaired the superior council, a governing body and court. Control over diplomatic relations and military affairs were given to the commandant general, who held office in Quebec City. The men who occupied these positions always clashed, presumably over the struggle for power and money. To help spur population growth in the colony, the king sent to New France seven hundred seventy-five single women, aged fifteen to thirty, called the king's daughters. Marriages with the Indians were encouraged, and indentured servants, known as engages, were sent by the Crown. Augustin de Saffray de Mesy was the first Commandant General and Jean Talon arrived in 1665 as the intendant, along with a French garrison of troops. In 1666, Ville-Marie (Montreal) had five hundred eighty-two inhabitants. A census conducted by Talon in 1666 showed a population of 3,215 in the whole of New France. Men outnumbered women two to one. Pierre Le Moyne d'Iberville, one of the most famous sons of New France and father of Louisiana, was born in Ville-Marie in 1661.

In 1673, Intendant Talon sent a French Canadian, Louis Jolliet and a Frenchman, Father Jacques Marquette to explore the Mississippi, Ohio, and Missouri rivers and claim the territory for France. The two explorers left Lake Michigan with two pirogues and five Canadians. They documented native villages as they descended the river and were guests of the Illinois nation. They followed the "Great River" down to the Arkansas River and turned back. They mapped the region, and Jolliet returned to Quebec to report his findings.

With the blessing of King Louis XIV in 1679, Robert de LaSalle began his exploratory expedition down the Mississippi

River from Quebec with his partner, Henri de Tonti to further his fur trading enterprise. He came among the Illinois nation and built the first French fort in that part of the New World called Fort Crevecaeur. LaSalle left Tonti in command of the fort, sailed to the mouth of the Mississippi in 1682, claimed the entire drainage basin of the Mississippi River for France, and named it *Louisiane*, in honor of Louis XIV. On his return voyage up the Mississippi, LaSalle founded Fort St. Louis on the Illinois River and abandoned Fort Crevecaeur. He left Tonti in command of Fort St. Louis as he decided to travel back to France by way of Quebec for ships and supplies.

In 1684, with backing from the Crown, LaSalle set sail from France with a large expedition of ships and supplies in order to find the mouth of the Mississippi by way of the Gulf of Mexico. Not knowing any landmarks, he went beyond the mouth westward, disembarked, made a small fort, and decided to find the great river by way of land. Unable to find the river, his men mutinied, and LaSalle was killed. Tonti traveled down the Mississippi from the Fort St. Louis to the mouth to meet LaSalle at the expected time of arrival. Not finding him, Tonti decided to return to the post. He traveled some ways up the Arkansas River, met with the Arkansas tribe, and made peace. He established a post on the Arkansas and left ten men. In the summer of 1686, Tonti received a land grant and a trading concession on the Arkansas in hopes of establishing a trading post to exchange beaver furs for French goods. In 1685, New France had a population of about 10,500 habitants as compared to about 160,000 in New England.

By 1688, New France's population was 11,562 people, made up primarily of fur traders, missionaries, and farmers settled mostly along the St. Lawrence Valley and on the banks of the Mississippi River. To help overcome its severe shortage of servants and laborers, King Louis XIV granted New France's petition to import black slaves from West Africa. While slavery was prohibited in France, it was permitted in the colonies as a means of providing the labor force needed to clear land, construct buildings, and, in the Caribbean colonies, work sugarcane plantations. The Code Noir of 1685 set the conditions by which slavery was allowed to exist. It required that all slaves be instructed as Catholics and prohibited any Protestant teachings. It expelled all Jews from the colony. It dealt with the treatment of slaves by their masters and the punishment of slaves for offenses, including running away.

Chapter Five

After the death of King Charles I of Spain in 1558, the Spanish Habsburgs were ruled by a succession of Philips: Philip II, Philip III, Philip IV and finally, Charles II became king in 1665, the only surviving son of Philip IV. He was born with physical and mental disabilities due to the constant inbreeding of first cousins and uncles, aunts, nieces and nephews within the Habsburg dynasty. When his father died and he ascended to the throne, Charles II was only four years of age. His mother, Mariana of Austria, another Habsburg, was made regent. In 1679 at the age of eighteen, Charles II married Marie Louise d'Orleans, eldest daughter of Philippe I, Duke of Orleans, the son of King Louis XIII of France. Marie died without having children at the age of twenty-five and Charles did not father an heir with his second wife, either. Charles II died on November 1, 1700 in Madrid, Spain.

The leaders of the European empires had long anticipated Charles II's death without an heir. His death without children ended the Spanish line of the Habsburgs dynasty. The Austrian Habsburgs did not take lightly the possibility of losing the entire Spanish empire, including its vast holdings in the New World. England was against the union of the French and Spanish Empires, too. Such a union would make France the leading world power and France would monopolize the Spanish trade with the New World. However, England and France were opposed to any claim that the Holy Roman Emperor Leopold I of the Austrian branch of the Habsburg dynasty had to the Spanish empire. Much diplomacy took place between the heads of state to resolve the problem but to no avail. Before his death, Spanish nobility convinced King Charles II of Spain to name Philippe de France, Duke of Anjou, and grandson of Charles II's sister, Maria Theresa of Spain, as his sole heir. Maria Theresa was the daughter of Philip IV, King of Spain and was the present Queen of France as the wife of Louis XIV. Philippe de France, the Duke of Anjou was the son of King Louis XIV's eldest son, Louis de France, Dauphin of France. Of course, the Sun King wanted his grandson named the King of Spain and he broke off all negotiations with England and Leopold. King Louis XIV realized, as did the other world leaders, that France would be the largest and strongest world kingdom with his grandson ruling Spain and his son, the heir apparent of France, eventually ruling the country. Such a coup would greatly disturb the balance of power, as it existed in the New and Old Worlds in 1700.

On November 24, 1700, shortly after Charles II died, Louis XIV proclaimed his grandson, Philippe de France, Duke of Anjou as Philip V, King of Spain. The new king was ordained the ruler of the entire Spanish empire. In 1701, because of Louis XIV's coup, the world was at war again with the beginning of the War of the Spanish Succession, only a few years after the conclusion of the Nine Year's War in 1697. The war was fought mostly in Europe. But French and English colonists sparred in North and South America and the West Indies in a conflict known to them as Queen Anne's War. The war began slowly as Leopold I of the Austrian Habsburg dynasty made claim to the Spanish throne. When Louis XIV began to expand his territorial possessions in Spain, the English, Portuguese, and Dutch entered the war on the side of the Holy Roman Empire against France and Spain. All sides began to raise armies and the war became a huge financial burden on all of the kingdoms. All sides suffered massive casualties. The war continued through the death of Louis XIV's son, Louis de France on April 14, 1711, heir apparent of the French throne.

The war on the high seas saw treasure ships targeted. Fighting raged in the New World. French, English, and Spanish fleets were all active in the West Indies. Acadia and the frontier between French Canada and the English Province of Massachusetts Bay were hotly contested. French militia and their native Indian allies made numerous raids on the outlying communities in Massachusetts. English militia made repeated attempts to capture Port-Royal and Acadia without success. Queen Anne of Great Britain finally funded a major naval expedition, and Acadia was captured in 1710. The war between France and England finally ended with the signing of the Treaty of Utrecht in 1713. The war concluded between France and Austria in 1714 with the Treaties of Rastatt and Baden. King Philip V was formally recognized as King of Spain and was forced to renounce his line of succession to the French Kingdom. Philip V retained the Spanish empire in the New World also. Italy was ceded to Austria. No important changes were made to the French Kingdom in Europe. France ceded control over Rupert's Land (the entire drainage basin of the Hudson Bay) and the Island of Newfoundland to Great Britain. Of the gravest of concerns to New France, France also ceded control over Acadia to the English. The French Canadians felt abandoned and English reprisals began. France and Spain, now both under Bourbon rulers, remained allies. This was the beginning of France's unraveling in the New World, but it ushered in a long period of peace among the nations.

"I will let myself out," Francois told the old guard once the visit with Pierre had ended. He hurried from the jailhouse.

Henri and Landis were waiting in the carriage. Francois decided not to say a word about what he had just learned, not even to Henri.

Embezzlement of the king's finances could cause one to lose his head. Francois knew Antoine Patin would receive his just reward, but it would be on the day of Francois's choosing.

They returned to Avery's office and discovered, to their horror that the trial was set for Friday, April 19. The magistrate was adamant about proceeding with criminal charges. They had only three days to secure Pierre's freedom. The three men left for Paris with the letter of introduction immediately. The distance from Amiens to Paris was some forty leagues, and a full day's ride by carriage. Francois had Landis stop at the Cathedral of Amiens to say an Our Father and a Hail Mary for the success of their enterprise.

On the way to Paris, Francois and Henri spoke business before taking up a conversation about the Regent of France and John Law.

"I heard the regent moved the Crown and his court back to Paris from Versailles. They entertain constantly. I even heard that they have drunken orgies in the Palais-Royal, and John Law is right in the thick of things," said Henri.

"Yes, Law seems to be a seedy character," replied Francois. "His smooth tongue has gained him access to the French nobility and the ear of the regent. Do you know he was born in Scotland? He is not even French, but he is well versed in finance and convinced the regent of a paper money scheme to save France from financial ruin."

"I know. Law was granted a twenty-year monopoly for a General Bank in 1716 and issued shares of stock as a publicly traded company. I thought about buying a couple of shares at the initial subscription price of five thousand livres. Only twelve hundred shares were offered, you know, and Law bought a quarter of them himself, and the king purchased three hundred eighty shares. I didn't buy. Then he started printing paper banknotes. Unfortunately, gullible as I am, I did deposit my silver and gold specie in exchange for its banknotes as everyone else did. And now these banknotes are nearly worthless," said Henri.

"I cannot understand how John Law then convinced the regent to nationalize the General Bank in December of 1718 and order its banknotes acceptable by the royal treasury. In effect law managed to withdraw all gold and silver out of circulation and left the royal treasury responsible for these banknotes. Arnaud told me that when the Crown bought all of the shares of Law's General Bank, initial investors made out well—up to 60 percent profit. We missed out," said Francois.

"John Law maintained management of the royal bank through the Mississippi Company after it was nationalized. And to think that all of our tax farm receipts now pass through the royal bank. Luckily, we bought shares in the Mississippi Company," said Henri. "I still own my fifty shares. I started buying them at the initial offering price of five hundred livres with you."

"I bought with you at the initial offering price, but I also bought some later at one thousand and two thousand livres as well, all with banknotes. I think the price is now around ten thousand livres per share. Arnaud suggests we sell them because of the current price fluctuation. I think I will sell my one hundred fifty shares," said Francois.

"The price per share was at fifteen thousand livres at the beginning of this year," replied Henri. "We missed the peak."

Francois agreed with him on that as well. "The shares have to retain some value especially with all the monopolies the Mississippi Company obtained from the Crown. It not only has the exclusive privilege of trading with the Louisiana colony, the company also holds the monopoly of the beaver skin trade with Canada, controls all gold and silver mines in Nouvelle France, and owns all of the lands, coasts, ports, and rivers in the Louisiana colony.

"Can you believe that the company has even acquired the monopoly on the tobacco trade? It controls the Senegal slave trade, trade with China, and the South Seas, too" said Henri.

"Yes, but his final stroke of genius was when the company acquired the Crown's coin mintage and our tax farm revenue streams. How could the Company not be worth ten thousand livres per share?" asked Francois.

"It does have many obligations, though. Its charter requires it to transport six thousand settlers and three thousand slaves to the colony, to build churches, and to provide clergymen. The charter allows it to wage war against the Indians and make peace treaties, make land grants, raise an army, construct forts, establish a judicial system, and appoint the commandant general of the colony," said Henri.

Francois knew that Bienville was the present commandant general, and that he'd been appointed for a second term after Crozat petitioned the Crown to be relieved of his monopoly in Louisiana in 1717. Though the colony must not have been as profitable as most believed if Crozat, a clever businessman, had abandoned his monopoly.

"We should be very careful with this paper money they disguise as banknotes," warned Henri.

"That's what I have been saying all along," said Francois.

"When we sell our stock in the Mississippi Company, we should convert the paper banknotes to coinage from the taxes we collect. We'll just turn in the banknotes instead," said Henri.

"Good idea. And maybe we can purchase additional parcels of land," said Francois.

"But prices for everything have gone so high. John Law keeps on printing banknotes. The whole kingdom is clamoring to purchase Mississippi Company stock with the influx of all this new paper money," said Henri.

"Then maybe we should hoard our gold and silver coinage for the time being," said Francois. "Not to change the subject, but I hope we have the chance to see Emily in Paris."

"Those are two good ideas, Francois. We must call on her if we have the time. I'm getting hungry. Let's stop at the next village," said Henri.

Pierre Le Moyne d'Iberville, the father of the Louisiana colony, was born in Ville-Marie, Canada on July 20, 1661, the same year Louis XIV began to personally rule France. Iberville's father, Charles Le Moyne, came to New France at the age of fifteen in 1641 as an indentured servant of the Jesuits, serving on Huron and Iroquois missions. He helped the settlers of Ville-Marie defend the city on numerous occasions from attacks by the Indians. Because he knew their language, Charles eventually became an emissary to the Indians on behalf of the commandant general of New France. His services to the Crown were rewarded by large land grants in Ville-Marie. Charles was active in the lucrative fur trade and was bestowed the rank of nobility in 1682. Iberville's father was reputed to be one of the wealthiest citizens in Ville-Marie at his death in 1685.

Iberville had two sisters and eleven brothers. His most famous brother was Jean-Baptiste Le Moyne, d'Bienville. All of his brothers rose to military fame in Canada and some died in battle. Iberville learned to sail at an early age and became a great seafarer. His military career in the service of New France began in 1686 when he took part in an expedition against the English posts in the Hudson Bay region. The English Crown granted a charter to the Hudson Bay Company to exploit the fur trade with the Indians. The French were determined to drive them out. In Europe in 1688, King Louis XIV started the Nine Years' War (also called The War of the Grand Alliance), which pitted France against England, Spain, and the Holy Roman Empire. Iberville spent the next ten years fighting with the English using ruthless tactics he learned from the Indians. His military successes eventually landed him a monopoly of the fur trade in the Hudson Bay by the Crown. He renamed a captured English fort to Fort Bourbon and the Indians were bringing in boatloads of pelts in exchange for French goods. Iberville made several trips to France during this period as he had gained the ear of the Crown.

After tiring from his exploits in the northern country and the harsh conditions of its winters, he was called upon to attack the English along the disputed New England- Acadia boundary. He had learned a good deal about the profits being made by

English and French fishermen exploiting the Grand Banks and he took advantage. He eventually captured and plundered the English fort of St. John on Newfoundland and raided, looted, and burned the smaller hamlets. As with most successful French campaigns in Nouvelle French, Louis XIV was so preoccupied with war in Europe that he would never reinforce and hold the ground gained by his French Canadians. The English on the other hand would reestablish their possessions with reinforcements after each victory.

The Treaty of Ryswick, signed on September 20, 1697, settled the Nine Years' War. France was confirmed the owner of the St. Lawrence, Acadia, and Saint-Domingue. (Acadia would be given to the English as spoils at the end of the War of the Spanish Succession in 1713.) Saint-Domingue was a French colony on the Caribbean island of Hispaniola. Spain controlled the entire island of Hispaniola from the 1490s until the second half of the 1600s, when French pirates began to establish bases on the western portion of the island. In the treaty, Spain formally recognized French control of the western third of the island. Saint-Domingue would become one of the richest and most prosperous French colonies in the West Indies. Saint-Domingue became an important port for France in the New World. It received numerous goods and products flowing to and from Europe. The fighting among the world powers stopped temporarily around 1700. Iberville returned to France in November of 1697, managing to retain his lucrative monopoly of the fur trade at Fort Bourbon until 1699.

The expansionist policies of Louis XIV heated up during the 1690s and he wished to contain the British to the east of the Appalachian Mountains. Impressed by his accomplishment in Hudson Bay and his other Canadian campaigns, France's Minister of Marine, Pontchartrain, chose Iberville to find the mouth of the Mississippi River. The chief objective was to find the mouth, select a good site to defend it, and block entry into the river by other nations. Iberville's younger brother, Jean-

Baptiste Le Moyne, d'Bienville, born on February 23, 1680 in Canada, was to accompany Iberville.

The two explorers left Brest, France in October 1698 with four ships. The exposition was composed of two frigates, the *Marin* and *Badine*, each carrying thirty guns. Compte de Surgeres commanded the *Marin*. Iberville commanded the *Badine*. With two smaller vessels, the fleet carried nearly two hundred colonists and a company of marines. Among the colonists were many women and children, the families of soldiers. They sailed first to Saint-Domingue, then north to Florida and west along the shores of the Gulf of Mexico until they reached a bay that they named Saint Louis. They made soundings along the gulf shore for possible French harbor sites. On January 31, 1699, Iberville anchored near Ship Island, took two long boats, and discovered the mouth of the Mississippi. He ascended the river nearly one hundred leagues until he encountered the Houmas Indians who confirmed LaSalle's presence and confirmed that he was in fact on the Mississippi River. He saw European goods in the possession of the Indians. Upon his return to the fleet, Iberville sent his brother, Bienville, down the Mississippi to sound the three passes at the mouth of the river. Iberville, with a few companions, returned to Ship Island by way of the Manchac (or *pass*), which connected the Mississippi River with Lakes Maurepas and Pontchartrain, a shortcut the Indians had shown him. This bayou was initially called Bayou Iberville and years later, Bayou Manchac. Upon his return to the coast, he built Fort Maurepas on the mainland at Biloxi Bay, which consisted of a simple fort and a few houses. On May 4, 1699, Iberville sailed for France, leaving behind a garrison of eighty-one men, women, and children, and his brother Bienville. Sauvolle was appointed commandant general and Bienville was second in command. Upon Sauvolle's sudden death in 1701, Beinville was appointed commandant general of the Louisiana colony.

Iberville recommended to the Crown immediate colonization and exploration of Louisiana, not necessarily for the

Crown's benefit. Why would any explorer risk his life, family, and possessions but for fame or fortune? The Crown's most pressing reason was the imminent English migration from the Carolinas. Yet, the king could not formally commit to the project for fear of offending the Spanish who were Louis XIV's ally in the quandary of the Spanish Succession. Furthermore, the Spanish crown had made claim of the Mississippi River. A second exploratory voyage was eventually approved, principally for the discovery of gold and silver mines and other resources.

Iberville left France in October 1699 and arrived in Biloxi on January 8, 1700. Iberville built a second fort on Mobile Bay to keep the English from descending the Mobile River from the mountains of Appalachia. He built another fort on the banks of the Mississippi, on learning from Sauvolle that two English armed ships had entered the Mississippi to establish a colony. These ships sailed back to the Gulf after encountering French ships and after being informed that they were on the Mississippi and were trespassers on French territory. On his way up the river, he selected the site for the new fort twenty-eight leagues from the mouth, and a short distance below the English Reach (English Turn). He concluded a treaty of peace with the village of the Natchez after finding they were the most civilized of all the Indian nations. Bienville was placed in command of the new fort on the Mississippi River with a force of twenty-five men. In May of 1700, Iberville once more set sail to France. While in Europe, King Louis XIV started the War of the Spanish Succession in the early part of 1701.

On his third trip to the colony, Iberville set sail from France on September 29, 1701 and arrived in Biloxi in December 1701, with orders to found a naval base at Mobile amongst the Indians of that name. Hostilities with the English were on the increase due to the war. He also established a deep water port on nearby Dauphin Island for the benefit of the colony, as Mobile Bay and the Mobile River were too shallow for sea-going vessels. He also had orders to implement a strong Indian policy. He once again brought a large amount of supplies, arms, and a number of colonists. Iberville was informed that the commandant general of Louisiana, Sauvolle, had died of yellow fever so Bienville was named Commandant General of Louisiana in 1701. Bienville remained commandant general until 1713. The colonists had been reduced by sickness to one hundred fifty in number. Bienville built a modest fort at Mobile called Fort Saint Louis, some forty leagues up the Mobile River in 1702. The first site being prone to flooding, they moved the fort south at the confluence of Mobile Bay and the Mobile River. This was the first capital of the Louisiana colony.

Iberville had learned a great deal while living with the Indians in Canada. He envisioned a French alliance with and between all of the Indian tribes that lived between the Mississippi River and the Appalachians, all in opposition to the British. The Carolina fur traders had encouraged the Chickasaw, a large Indian tribe on the east bank of the Mississippi between the Arkansas River and the Appalachians, to war against the French. The Chickasaw wanted the same trade terms and gifts provided by the British. Iberville made peace with the Choctaw, who lived between the Chickasaw and the gulf coast on the east side of the Mississippi River. They became his allies. He also attempted a treaty between the Chickasaw and Choctaw. He put an end to the slave trade raids on the Indian tribes promoted by the British. He resolved conflicts between the Homas, Bayougoula, Tunica, and Natchez. He realized that contact with the Indians and mingling with them was a necessity. He encouraged missionaries to live with the Indians. He had young French boys fourteen to fifteen years of age to live with the Indian tribes to learn their language. They would later become a corps of interpreters for the French.

Tensions rose between the Commandant General of Canada, Vaudreuil, and Iberville over control of the colony, especially over the beaver skin trade. The Commandant General of Canada wanted the administration over all of New France. Iberville wanted to split it up with Iberville having control of Louisiana. The Commandant General of Canada accused Iberville of exploiting the Louisiana fur trade for the benefit of his family. Iberville was rumored to have traded for a large haul of beaver skins from the Indians and courtiers de bois and sold them in Quebec on one of his return trips to France. In any event, Minister Pontchartrain followed Iberville's advice and appointed a clerk to receive furs on the lower Mississippi.

On his fourth trip to Louisiana in 1706, Iberville was put in charge of a fleet of twelve vessels with over two thousand regular troops, colonial militia, and Canadians. His orders were to harass the British in the West Indies. He began by capturing several islands, including Nevis. His campaign through the West Indies would have been ruthless had it not been for his sudden death in July 1706 in Havana. Iberville never made the fourth trip to his beloved Louisiana. Iberville had become wealthy. He had purchased a lucrative cocoa plantation on Saint-Domingue and a large farm and residence in France valued at ninety thousand livres. The death of Iberville left a void in the Louisiana colony that only his brother, Bienville, could fill.

Chapter Six

At the height of Louis XIV's power, New France consisted of a huge expanse of the North American continent. It included the entire drainage basin of the Mississippi River between the Rocky Mountains and the Appalachian Mountains. The Gulf of Mexico was its southern boundary. It also included the several islands in the Caribbean, including Saint-Domingue , the five Great Lakes, the Hudson Bay into northern Canada, the St. Lawrence River drainage basin, Acadia, and Newfoundland. The capital was Quebec City and one commandant general and one intendant ruled the vast empire for the French Crown. New France had been divided into five administrative districts: Canada, Acadia, Hudson Bay, Newfoundland and Louisiana. Louisiana was divided into two regions: Upper Louisiana (Haute–Louisiane or the Illinois Country) and Lower Louisiana (Basse–Louisiane). Lower Louisiana included the Arkansas Post and all territories south to the Gulf of Mexico. Each district had a commandant general and an intendant (commissaire ordinaire). The commissaire ordonnateur was the chairman of the Superior Council, the governing body in each administrative district.

However, the end of the War of the Spanish Succession in 1713, and the eventual death of King Louis XIV in 1715, brought change to the New World. The Treaty of Utrecht in 1714 ceded the Acadia peninsula, the Hudson Bay area and Newfoundland to England. France retained its other New World possessions, including the Colony of Louisiana and Canada. With the transfer of land, the English immediately treated the French Acadians harshly from the outset. They forbade the Acadians to leave Acadia for fear of providing reinforcements to the New France militia. They also used the Acadians' industry to provide food for the British troops. They also deprived them of their land and freedom of worship. Acadia was renamed by the English to Nova Scotia (New Scotland).

After a reign of seventy-two years, Louis XIV died of gangrene at Versailles on September 1, 1715, four days before his seventy-seventh birthday. The Sun King had become the longest serving king in Europe and the most powerful in France at his death but left no surviving sons. Louis XIV's great-grandson would become the next King of France.

Francois was jolted awake by a sudden stop of their carriage. He was having nightmares about Pierre, locked up in the king's prison. In them, Pierre was in chains for life and an evil spirit was prodding him with a red-hot poking iron. Francois's abrupt awaking was a somewhat refreshing moment until he realized where he was—a reality not too far outside his nightmares. Outside the carriage window, it was dark.

"Where in the hell are we Landis?" screamed Francois.

"We are on the outskirts of Paris, sir," came Landis's reply.

"Well, why have we stopped?" asked Francois.

"We are coming up to a checkpoint by the royal guard. The horses are very tired. I stopped a minute to relieve myself," said Landis.

The night air still had a cool dampness, left over from the proceeding winter. The sky was dotted by brightly shining stars beckoning a sojourner's attention, but the distant lights of Paris were on everyone's minds.

"Let's get going. Once we get through the checkpoint, follow the Seine River and head to Notre Dame Cathedral. I think there is an inn near there," said Francois.

Landis hurriedly returned to his post on the carriage seat. The rest stop had been an immediate relief, but the thought of a meal and a nice soft bed after his long day of driving the carriage excited him. The checkpoint went easily and Landis made his way on the King's Highway along the banks of the Seine into Paris. The streets turned from dirt into cobblestone once inside the city. The clacking of the horse and carriage rang out as he passed the huge Notre Dame Cathedral. A few blocks from the church he came upon the Fleur-de-lis Inn, its sign prominently hanging over the front door. The façade was made of stone, and candlelight shone through several windows of the four-story building, including the front entrance. Directly across the street was the Mermaid Tavern, where several people were milling around outside. The place seemed full. Landis stopped in front of the Fleur-de-lis Inn.

"This will do, Landis," shouted Francois as he exited the carriage. "Help us with the baggage and then find a livery stable for the horses and carriage."

As Francois was grabbing a bag from Landis, a porter came out of the inn. "Let me get that for you monsieur. Will you be staying with us for some time?" asked the porter.

"This night and maybe another," said Francois as he gave the bag to the porter. "Landis! Henri and I will register with the innkeeper. Here is some livre for boarding the horses. It is now nine p.m. Meet us back here in thirty minutes when you finish." Francois turned to the porter. "Is there a livery stable near here?"

"Yes, monsieur. We are here on Boulevard Saint-Germain. Go two blocks and turn right on Rue Monge. You will find a livery there," said the porter.

Landis returned to the inn and, upon inquiry with the innkeeper, he discovered to his delight that his traveling companions were across the street at the Mermaid Tavern. Landis wasted no time in joining them.

"Landis, come join us," shouted Francois over the constant roar of the patrons. "Here is a bite of supper and a pint of ale. Meet Mr. Lancelot, our new friend. He has been telling us the latest news about King Louis XV and his court."

The tavern was nearly full with patrons. The piano player was running off tunes and the many merry mermaids were hurriedly filling orders for spirits of various sorts while at the same time comforting the gawking eyes of their intoxicated patrons. Tobacco smoke filled the room. The whole place had an unnatural feel about it.

"Lancelot says that Bienville is in Paris," said Henri.

"Who is Bienville?" asked Landis.

"Why, he is the Commandant General of the Louisiana colony. If Canada had a child, its name would be Louisiana and Bienville would be the father," explained Lancelot.

"I think I might like to go to the Louisiana colony," said Landis.

"What would we do without you here?" asked Henri and everyone laughed in a drunken frenzy.

"John Law and his Mississippi Company are constantly looking for poor souls to send over. What I hear, they are very short handed in their labor force," said Lancelot.

"Who is this fellow, John Law?" asked Landis.

"The Scottish slob from Edinburgh running this kingdom," said Lancelot. "Back in England, he wanted to start a system of issuing paper money, but the monarch wouldn't have anything to do with it. They say he was run out of England when his father died. He supposedly killed a man in a duel. He inherited a large sum from his father and squandered it with all of the elite of Europe. He mostly gambled, drank, and chased women throughout Europe until he landed here. He somehow fell right in with the regent, and now they are running the kingdom into ruin, and the Louisiana colony along with it."

"I think I shall turn in," said François. "We have a long day tomorrow."

Landis and Henri rose to follow Francois back to the inn. They were all very tired now that they had eaten a bite and drank a considerable amount of ale.

"I think I may have a little more conquering to do," said Lancelot as he glanced over to a buxom merry maiden.

Francois rose early the next morning before dawn. Paris was still quiet from the hustle and bustle of the previous night. The small candle he lit barely provided enough light in his tiny room. As he washed his face from the lava beau and began to shave, he could hear the roosters—the trumpeters of the morning sun—crowing in the distance from his open window. It immediately reminded him of home and his faithful wife, Marie. The horror of Pierre in prison shuddered through his body to the point of making him sick with nausea. He thought it might have been the consequences of the ale the previous night. But thoughts of Pierre's release restored his fortitude. Francois immediately regained control of his thoughts and body and planned out his day. The plan was simple: gain release for Pierre from the Minister Guillaume Dubois or from Regent Philippe II himself.

Francois finally awakened Henri and Landis. Landis went to get the carriage as Henri and Francois packed their things and settled the bill with the innkeeper. Landis drove up with the horses and carriage just as they stepped outside.

"Take us to Notre Dame Cathedral. I need to stop and say a prayer for a successful trip," said Francois to Landis. Landis knew where to go as he had passed near the church the night before. He pulled the carriage up to the front of the five-hundred-year-old church with its two tall bell towers, a huge rose window, and the three arches towering over them. Landis never got to church that much. He immediately decided to say a prayer himself when he saw a gargoyle staring down at him with a devilish gaze. He hurriedly tied the horses to a hitching post and followed Francois and Henri into the church.

The petite wooden chairs and kneelers paled in comparison to the ornate vaulted ceiling and the enormous stained glass windows that surrounded the interior. The church's grandeur immediately put them in their place. Landis fathomed that he and his two companions were only three of God's little creatures in a much more complicated world. Their prayers somehow relieved their fears and stoked their confidence in their mission.

Landis made the short drive to the Palais–Royal and was ordered to stay with the carriage as Francois and Henri went in to receive the forgiveness for which they had prayed. The palace was a grand, two-story structure made of brick with massive columns across the front. Francois and Henri entered into a majestic foyer.

"We are here to see Minister Guillaume Dubois," said Francois to a courtier. "I am the king's tax collector from Picardy Province. Please give him this letter of introduction from a mutual friend of ours, Advocate Avery Legard."

The courtier took the letter of which the life of Pierre so depended. "Please wait here," ordered the courtier as he disappeared behind a colossal set of double bronze doors. Francois and Henri could not stand still with the nervous energy inside them. They passed the wait, which seemed like hours to them, gawking at the ornate foyer. The domed ceiling, painted with Greek and Roman gods in brilliant colors, overwhelmed their senses. They stared back at the human-like Greek and Roman statues that gazed at them from centuries past. Marble busts of past kings, including King Louis XIV, lined one wall as if protecting the kingdom he once ruled. Enormous paintings of the royals hunting in country scenes decorated the walls.

The courtier delivered the letter to Chief Minister Dubois. Minister Dubois had been tutor to young Philippe II as the future regent was growing up. Minister Dubois had been around the regent all of his life. He ascended from lowly beginnings and worked hard to secure his present position. As chief minister to the regent, he wielded considerable sway. In addition to the influence he possessed in the royal court, he had accumulated a large financial stash for himself. Most of it was from ill-gotten gains from his cronies in the government, one being Antoine Patin. Minister Dubois and Antoine Patin knew each other from childhood. Minister Dubois aided all of his friends even if the assistance was a detriment to the kingdom. As a reward for getting him his taxing district, Antoine Patin had been skimming the tax collections and paying his benefactor, Minister Dubois, part of the illicit take.

"He must be here about his son," said the minister as he took the letter from the courtier. He pondered its contents a long while before fabricating his approach to the regent. The schemes concocted to cover a guilty conscious often weighed on the soul of those whose identity is obscured by confusion and delusion. Chief Minister Dubois approached the regent.

"I just received a letter from Avery Legard, an advocate in Amiens. He is requesting leniency for a one, Pierre Mayeux, the individual I mentioned to you earlier this morning, who is accused of robbing Antoine Patin, our tax farmer in the Northern provinces. The boy's father, Francois Mayeux, our tax collector from Picardy Province, just delivered the letter to me in person. He is waiting in the foyer," said Minister Dubois to the regent. "They are requesting the king's pardon."

"Well, what shall we do with him?" asked the regent. "We cannot reward thievery even if he is the son of one of our tax collectors, especially if the crime is against another of our tax collectors. Did you get all of the facts of the robbery? Is he guilty?"

"Antoine Patin sent me notice by rider last evening that his driver saw the young Mayeux boy at the scene of the robbery. The boy is being held at the prison in Amiens," said Minister Dubois.

"What do I know of these tax collectors? Do as you will. I suggest punishment of three years in the king's prison. Such an offense would normally require his life. Draft a letter under my seal to the Magistrate of the Parlement of Amiens," ordered the regent as he went about his breakfast.

Minister Dubois did not achieve his position in the Royal Court for being an imbecile. He also received word from Antoine Patin that a second set of books was taken in the robbery. Minister Dubois knew very well that all taxes generated in the provinces were the king's property. If this skimming scheme became public, not only his career but also his life would quickly end. He had to get possession of those ledgers.

"Please have Monsieur Mayeux come into my chambers," said Minister Dubois to the courtier.

The courtier found Francois and Henri pacing in the foyer just as he had left them. "Please follow me," said the courtier. "Minister Dubois wishes to see only you, Monsieur Mayeux."

"You stay here, Henri. I will be right back," said Francois.

The interior of the palace was just as ornate as the foyer. Francois soon realized just where all of his tax collections were going: the king's palace. He was directed to the minister's lavish chambers and walked in.

"You have something in your possession of importance to Monsieur Antoine Patin," said the minister without delay.

"Do you mean his ledger books?" asked Francois. "I have not seen them."

"I want them back. The regent has decided not to grant leniency to your son. Yet, I have decided his sentence. It is contained in this letter to Magistrate Reynard under the regent's seal. Have those ledgers back to me within two weeks or else. That will be all."

Francois was shocked. He reappeared from behind the towering double doors with a grim appearance as if he had died, gone to hell, and come back again. The encounter with Chief Minister Dubois did not materialize as imagined.

"Have you spoken to him?" asked Henri. "You look like you just saw the spawn of Satan himself."

"I did," said Francois. "Dubois has given me a royal decree under the seal of the regent himself. But Dubois did not tell me the damned decision. I dare not open it. He addressed it to Magistrate Reynard. We must get to Amiens at once."

As Francois began to settle his nerves, a large crowd of people entering the Palais-Royal again disturbed his relative tranquility. A tall, slender man walked in, encircled and followed by a number of men and women. The man was dressed in a royal blue coat hanging to his knees. Tight curls of a brown, parted wig huge to his shoulders. White stockings flattered the high-heeled boots on his feet. His followers attended to his needs as he walked with authority across the foyer and entered the double doors at the other end. His cohorts all entered as chicks following a mother duck. The clamor all began and ended in only a matter of seconds.

"Who the hell was that?" asked Francois to the courtier.

"Why, that was John Law, the Minister of Finance," said the courtier.

"He sure has become the rage of Paris," said Henri.

"The rage is not with him, but in me at the moment. Let's be gone from this dreadful place," said Francois.

The Louisiana colony had been in French possession for over forty years and was never profitable. In fact, it had been a drain on the treasury of the French Crown. Unlike Canada, the French Crown did not take control over the administration of the Louisiana colony and established a royal government. Instead, King Louis XIV granted a royal charter on September 14, 1712, to the merchant and nobleman, Antoine Crozat. The royal charter conceded Crozat exclusive control over all foreign and domestic trading privileges within the colony for fifteen years. The monopoly allowed Crozat the right to appoint all local officials, permission to work all mines, title to all unoccupied lands, control over agricultural production and manufacture, and sole authority over the African slave trade. In return he was obligated to send two ships of supplies and settlers annually and to govern the colony in accordance with French law. The Louisiana colony was not profitable. In fact Crozat loss just under 1 million livres, In August 1717 he petitioned the king and his ministers and was granted release from his monopoly. By 1717, the population of colonists in Louisiana numbered about five hundred. But the regent wanted to continue the search for the precious metals rumored to exist. So his friend and confidant, John Law, went to work acquiring a controlling interest in the now bankrupt Crozat monopoly, the Company of the West, which usually went by the name of the Mississippi Company.

Law convinced the regent to cede the entire Louisiana colony, which included the entire Mississippi River drainage basin, to the Mississippi Company in August of 1717. The Company was granted all the land, coasts, and rivers including all of the forts, ammunition and vessels in the Colony, the remnants of Crozat's monopoly. The Company was granted a twenty-five-year monopoly on trade with the colony including the profitable beaver fur trade in New France. The Company was allowed to build forts and garrison them with royal soldiers of the king. The Company could appoint all officers commissioned by the king; they could enter into treaties with the various Indian nations and call on the French government for military assistance at any time; they could also appoint its own commandant general and officers in the colony and could make land grants to potential developers. Law anointed himself director general and had several influential royals and merchants named as directors. The directors of the Company appointed Beinville as commandant general of the colony in September 1717. The Company was required to transport six thousand colonists and three thousand slaves before the end of its charter. It was also required to build churches and provide clergy under the authority of the Archbishop in Quebec City.

John Law financed the Mississippi Company's initial operations by the public offering of shares. The initial public offering began on September 14, 1717 at five hundred livres per share. By 1718, the Company owned several ships and had already made several voyages to the Louisiana colony. Law continued to grow the Mississippi Company through a series of mergers and acquisitions. The Company purchased the tobacco monopoly in August 1718, the Company of the Senegal in December of 1718, the Company of China in May 1719, The Company of Africa in July 1719, the right to run the royal mint in July 1719, and the right to collect all taxes in August 1719. In early 1720, the Company took over the Royal Bank, which Law had created, and bought the Company of Saint-Domingue with the monopoly on the slave trade with Guinea.

In January 1720, John Law became the Minister of Finance of France with the unimpeded blessing of the regent and Minister Dubois. He controlled all of France's finances, all of its ability to create money and all of its ability to collect taxes. Through the Mississippi Company, he controlled all of France's foreign trade and colonial development. Law paid for all of this by issuing additional paper shares in the Mississippi Company. These shares were bought with paper banknotes issued from his bank. As expected, the value of shares in the Mississippi Company climbed. Investors from across France and Europe clamored for stock ownership. By December 1719, share prices had reached ten thousand livres. By January 1720, the price of a share was near fifteen thousand livres. Law continued to issue banknotes to fund the purchase of additional shares in the Company. John Law had managed to create a national obsession in the Mississippi Company. Men sold all their possessions and moved to Paris to speculate on shares of the Mississippi Company. The French capital experienced an explosive growth of Frenchmen and foreigners alike. The influx of wealth also attracted vagabonds by the thousands into Paris. A huge financial bubble developed.

Shares were sold at the royal bank in Paris. Before the opening of the market, crowds would gather. At its peak, it was not uncommon for the royal police to close off the street in front of the bank. One side of the barricade would gather the farmers, shopkeepers, bakers, meat cutters and others of that estate. On the other side of the barricade, noblemen, cardinals, bishops, clergy, and courtiers of the king would gather. At the predetermined time, the obstacle was removed and all would mingle to trade stocks in the Mississippi Company. No matter your station in life, nobles with enormous fortunes or peasants who gathered enough investors together to buy one share, all would take part in the mayhem. Everyone wanted to buy or sell stock in the Mississippi Company. Fortunes were made and lost. Millionaires were created and destroyed. Such was the state of France in April 1720.

The prayers at Notre Dame Cathedral had not managed to change Francois' temperament toward the crown. Francois and Henry hurriedly returned to the waiting carriage with Landis at the reins. As they were exiting the Palais-Royal, Henri reminded Francois that they still had to sell their stock in the Mississippi Company and pay a visit to Emily before leaving Paris. Francois agreed, and told Landis to drive them to the Royal Bank.

The ride to the bank took only minutes. Landis seemed to become familiar with the city as he drove through the cobblestone streets. As he neared the royal bank, the street became more crowded with carriages and people to the point that the horses neared a crawl. Francois, still agitated with his encounter with Minister Dubois, hollered at Landis to stop. Henri retrieved the stock certificates from the strong box in the floor of the carriage and he and Francois exited.

"I am very glad that when we bought them, we stashed our stock certificates at the bank in Amiens for safekeeping," said Henri.

"Tie the horses to this hitching post and follow us," ordered Francois to Landis.

They began walking down the middle of the street toward the headquarters of the royal bank. The people on the street were packed like salted fish in a barrel. The sound of hollering could be heard in the near distance; Francois imagined the moderate roar sounded similar to that of spectators in the Roman Colosseum. Landis was trying to keep up while taking in all the sights and sounds: grand store fronts, gentlemen dressed in powdered wigs—he even thought one was wearing make-up, a spectacle a country boy may see only once in his lifetime.

He found a pamphlet on the ground and picked it up. Unable to read much, the only word he could recognize was *Louisiana*. He stuck the pamphlet into his pocket. They struggled through the crowds until they finally reached the front of the royal bank.

"We need to find a stock jobber," hollered Francois to Henri and Landis.

"What's a stock jobber?" asked Landis.

"He will be the fellow taking orders to buy and sell stocks," said Henri.

"Two hundred shares in the Mississippi Company at 12,500 livres a piece," offered Francois to a jobber that approached.

"Sold," shouted the jobber. "Give me your certificates and follow me."

Francois handed over the stock certificates with apprehension. He and Henri had accumulated those shares over the past two years by skimping and saving nearly all of their profits from the tax farm and buying two or three shares at a time. As he followed the jobber into the bank to settle the deal, he called back to Henri and Landis, "I'll meet you at the carriage."

Henri and Landis made it through the crowd and managed to find the carriage still parked where they had left it.

"Look what I found on the street," said Landis, showing Henri the pamphlet. "What does it say?"

"It's describing the Louisiana colony," said Henri as he began to read it to Landis. "The climate is such that the temperature hovers near springtime year round. The soil is so fertile just scratching and dropping seeds will grow an overflowing harvest. The lakes and rivers are teeming with fish so that one cast of the net will satisfy your needs for the year. Every fruit and vegetable known to man are everywhere for the picking. The forests are loaded with wild duck, deer, pheasants, and woodcock to satisfy the most discriminating of palettes. The Indians, who worship the white man as Gods, are at your service at a beck and call to perform the smallest of tasks. Most important of all, the land is strewn with gold and silver mines.

Dipping a lamb's wool into a rushing stream will produce a golden fleece. Lumps of gold and silver lay everywhere, just for the taking."

Landis could not wait any longer. An overwhelming feeling of joy and delight built within. The more Henri read the more Landis's eyes lit with pleasure. The idea that fish and wild game could be had freely by a poor peasant such as himself convinced him. "Henri, I must go to Louisiana," blurted out Landis.

"Landis! Landis," said Henri as if calling from a distant land. "These words are not true. They are tales to encourage emigrants to settle the colony and the public to buy the stock. John Law has flooded France with these flyers. Why, if these things were true, all of France would be in Louisiana. Did you not see the frenzy just a minute ago? I'm afraid John Law has produced a creature called Louisiana Colony from the mother of the beast, the Mississippi Company."

"Well, I still want to go. When are we leaving for Amiens?" asked Landis.

"Just as soon as Francois returns. If we leave now, we may get there by midnight and get a few hours of sleep. You know Pierre's court date is tomorrow," said Henri as he looked to the swarm of people and wondered how Francois was making out. Just then, he spotted a familiar figure in the crowd walking past. It was Emily, Pierre's sister.

"Emily!" cried Henri as he rushed through the mob to greet her.

"Henri, what are you doing in Paris?" asked Emily.

"Did you hear about Pierre?" asked Henri.

"Yes, it is awful," said Emily. "You know my husband, Leon, is a tax accountant for the royal bank. He told me Pierre's arrest was all the talk at the bank–the son of a tax farmer robbing another tax farmer. He was concerned that Father could loose his taxing district."

"Well, we have more important problems at the moment. We are trying to get Pierre out of prison. His trial is tomorrow, in Amiens. Your father is here. He is selling our stock in the Mississippi Company as we speak. If you will wait a minute, you can see him."

"Getting rid of those shares is a good decision," said Emily. "Leon says the Mississippi Company has acquired the entire debt of France by issuing bonds and paying the bondholders with banknotes and shares. Law has been manipulating the price of shares in the Mississippi Company by issuing new shares and paying inflated prices with banknotes. He is getting ready to devalue both the shares and banknotes by half. There are far too many banknotes in circulation. None are backed by gold and silver coins. He has created a huge financial bubble that will burst at any minute."

"That explains the sudden increase in prices for everything–too much paper money chasing too little produce and merchandise," reasoned Henri.

"How good to see you, Emily," said Francois as he walked up with a leather satchel in one hand.

"Father, it has been a while. What do you have there?"

"A bag full of banknotes," Francois said jokingly.

"You have a very smart daughter," said Henri. "She has just been explaining to me how the financial system of the kingdom is being run into the ground by John Law."

"You and Leon must come see your mother and I soon," said Francois. "She is in a terrible state with this predicament with Pierre. We are off to Amiens as we speak. Let us go."

As Francois placed the satchel in the strong box in the floor of the carriage, Emily opined to herself how rude it was of her father to be so flippant in his hasty departure. She always craved more attention from her father, more than she thought she received. She decided to write her mother that night.

Francois was not looking forward to the drive back to Amiens. The road was bumpy and the seats in the carriage got uncomfortable very quickly. The heat inside the carriage drenched their clothing with sweat and seemed to attract all the dust kicked up by the horses. Francois determined that the unpleasantness was a minor distraction compared to the suffering Pierre was experiencing. The three travelers were off again, this time heading north. The sun was shining brightly as they passed Notre Dame and over the Pont Neuf, the oldest bridge in Paris, to cross the Seine.

"I always seem to be running from one crisis to the next with my children," said Francois. "I never seem to slow down and have time to enjoy myself and my life with my wife."

"My children are the same way," said Henri. "They occupy so much of your time."

Francois began to reminisce about his life. He remembered his peasant parents, doing without the nothing they already had, hiding away every penny so he could get an education. Yet, he could never remember them showing him affection. He could not recall either parent ever telling him they loved him. His marriage to Marie was the happiest time he could remember.

His marriage was based more on circumstance and ambition than love and affection. Marie became pregnant while they were courting and they were married in haste. Her family ties allowed him to acquire his tax farm through the help of her father. He had overcome the odds and acquired his own business and a rapidly growing family in those early years. However, shortly after Marie became pregnant with Nicholas, his business pursuits always seemed to be the focal point of his life. Life for him had become all about learning the business. He never had any time for the family, even when Emily and Pierre were born.

A feeling of loneliness and rejection suddenly overcame him. He had not faced the constant worry over all of the family's obstacles as he was currently immersed. In fact, he realized that he had placed most of the burden on Marie and the children. His attention had always been directed to the tax farm, yet his love for Marie had sprouted, matured, and multiplied.

The carriage ride back to Amiens took until about midnight. Landis dropped his passengers off at the Boor's Nest Inn and stabled the horses and carriage at Karlis's Livery. They all turned in for the night in anticipation of Pierre's court date.

The next morning Francois was up early as usual. He made plans with Henri that he would visit his advocate, Avery Legard, before court and give him the letter that Minister Dubois had composed. Henri and Landis were to go to the Parlement of Amiens and wait on him and Legard. However, when he arrived at the advocate's office, the secretary explained that Mr. Legard would not be in the office this morning but was instead going directly to parlement. Francois headed for court with great anticipation. He needed to talk with Legard before the proceedings began to inform him what had transpired with Minister Dubois and the need to work out a plan of action with the magistrate. Unfortunately, providence had a mind of its own.

When Francois finally arrived at the Parlement of Amiens, a large crowd had already gathered in the courtroom. The large room was separated by the bar, a wall-like structure about waist high. The spectators had no seats and it was standing room only. The audience was standing behind the bar and everyone was talking about one case or another. Francois walked into a state of confusion, it seemed. Behind the bar was the bench for the magistrate. In one corner near the bench was a holding cell for prisoners, but Pierre was nowhere to be found. Hanging over the bench was a large portrait of Louis XIV. A painting of the young Louis XV had not yet made its arrival. Francois nervously gazed around the room in search of Advocate Legard, Henri, and Landis. Finally, he spotted Henri and Landis standing in the crowd and hurried over.

"Have you seen Mr. Legard yet?" asked Francois as he approached Henri. "He was not at his office." Francois was visibly shaken and had broken into a cold sweat.

"No, we haven't. We just arrived ourselves," said Henri. "Try to calm yourself."

Just then, a bailiff walked in from behind a door on one side of the bench to announce the magistrate's arrival and the formal beginning of the court proceedings. Francois, Henri, and Landis hurriedly shoved through the crowd to take a position just behind the bar. Following the magistrate into court was Advocate Legard.

"Oyez! Oyez! Oyez, the Parlement of the Most High, King of France, Louis XV, is now in session, the Honorable Magistrate Reynard presiding on this nineteenth day of April 1720. Peace, order, and quiet are hereby commanded. God save this court and our kingdom. Long live the king," barked the bailiff.

"The first order of business will be our criminal docket," said Magistrate Reynard in a slow, deliberate voice. His long, white powdered wig and dark crimson robe trimmed in gold embroidery displayed the noble duty of the king. "Bring in the prisoners."

As the prisoners were herded into the holding cell, Francois managed to capture the attention of Advocate Legard and gestured for him to come over. The shackles and chains of the prisoners clinked and clanked as they shuffled into position in the holding cell. The whole ritual made an awful noise. The crowd could only stare in amazement and thank God that they were not in those prisoners' shoes. Francois immediately caught the eye of Pierre. When Pierre saw his father, he lowered his head as if to sob in humiliation.

Francois whispered to Advocate Legard, "Thank God you are here. I have been looking for you all morning. You must give this letter from Minister Dubois to the magistrate before he decides Pierre's fate. I have no idea what is says."

"That is a frightening thought. I take the visit did not go well. I did speak to the magistrate this morning on Pierre's behalf. I must admit, he was not very pleased after reading the affidavit of Antoine Patin," whispered Legard.

"The clerk will read the docket," ordered the magistrate.

"Amo Bucher, please rise," said the clerk. "You have been charged with the murder of Larue Vasser on or about April 2, 1720 in that you stabbed him to death in a brawl inside the Lion's Gate Tavern."

"After reading the police report, I find you guilty as charged. Anything to say for yourself?" asked the magistrate.

"I was only trying to defend myself," hollered Amo Bucher.

"Your sentence shall be death by hanging in the morning," ordered the magistrate. A loud mumbling sound overcame the audience. The people of Amiens had not seen a good hanging for some weeks. Such a spectacle always drew a crowd. What really brought the whole town out, however, was the headman's axe. But beheadings were usually reserved for the nobility and Amo Bucher was not from the noble estate. Francois empathized with the poor soul and prayed that Pierre's sentence would not be as harsh.

"Next case," ordered the magistrate.

"Lovell Godard, please rise," said the clerk. "You have been charged with the theft of two shares of stock in the Mississippi Company from one, Aron Sully, on or about April 10, 1720."

"The affidavit against you, Mr. Godard, says you were caught trying to sell the shares to a butcher in Amiens. Your sentence shall be ten years in the king's prison. Next case," ordered the magistrate.

"Pierre Mayeux, please rise," said the clerk.

Pierre rose slowly from his seat. The eight days in prison had already taken a toll on his spirit as well as his physical body. Thoughts of being away from Simone and his family for an extended period of time ran through his mind and haunted his soul. Francois and Henri stared intently as the clerk read the charges. "You have been charged with the robbery of Antoine Patin, a tax collector in Picardy, on the night of April 11, 1720."

At this moment, Avery Legard sprang to his feet. "Magistrate Reynard, I have in my possession a letter under seal from the regent himself, the Duke of Orleans. As you are aware, Pierre Mayeux is the son of another tax collector from Picardy. May I approach the bench?"

Advocate Legard handed the letter to the magistrate. Magistrate Reynard broke the seal and began reading the letter to himself. Pierre, Francois, Henri, and Landis were all shaking like a long-tailed cat in a room full of rockers. The suspense was too much to bear. The magistrate took a long time reading the letter and making his decision.

"After reading the affidavit of Antoine Patin and his assistant and speaking with Advocate Legard, I shall follow the edict of the regent, even though King Louis XIV some years ago abandoned the idea of sending criminals to the colony. Pierre Mayeux, I find you guilty as charged. It is the decision of this court that you shall be banished to the Louisiana colony and listed as a prisoner on the passenger list of the *La Profond*. The ship will set sail to the Louisiana colony on June 10, 1720 from the port of La Rochelle, France. Make sure you are on that ship or else. You shall be released today," said Magistrate Reynard. "Next case."

The policy regarding slaves changed in 1717 when John Law and the Mississippi Company took over the Louisiana colony. Law's monopoly contract with the French Crown called for six thousand settlers and three thousand slaves to be transported to the colony. Under Louis XIV, if a slave touched French soil in Europe, he became free. The new policy stated that slaves remained a slave if they ever reached France. Many attempted freedom as stowaways on ships heading to France. An edict was passed that the merchant who brought the slave as a stowaway had to pay for his return. Louis XIV banned slavery in France during his reign, frowned upon slavery in the Louisiana colony, but allowed it as necessary evil in the Caribbean islands. Yet, a number of Indians became slaves despite the Crown's prohibition. These Indians were usually captured by the English during English raids and sold to the French. They were often sent to Saint-Domingue to work on the sugarcane plantations. The French planters in the Louisiana colony preferred African slaves because the Indians would run off and could live on their own in their native land where the slaves could not. In 1717, after Louis XIV's death, the regent and John Law decided to import African slaves into Louisiana to develop a plantation economy. The Mississippi Company eventually obtained the monopoly over the slave trade. Over half of the six thousand African slaves entering Louisiana arrived between 1719 and 1731.

Because of the lack of laborers in the colony and John Law's ineffectual advertising campaign promoting emigration, Regent

Philippe II issued several ordinances and decrees concerning criminals and vagabonds. By royal proclamation, all vagabonds were ordered to leave Paris or be subject to immediate arrest and deportation to the colony. Likewise, all criminals sentenced to the gallows or violators of the salt tax monopoly were deported to the Louisiana colony. Vagabonds and criminals were rounded up and sent to Louisiana in Law's ships by the hundreds. This lasted until May 9, 1720 when Bienville's protestations were finally heeded and a royal decree was issued that prohibited the transportation of vagabonds and criminals to the Louisiana Colony.

New France's legal system followed the codes and edicts of the Crown. It did not develop its own set of laws. The Superior Council in Quebec City recorded all land transactions, sales, civil, and criminal cases and successions and acted as a court of final jurisdiction. Initially it was the only court in the colony until posts grew in size to support a notary and magistrate to hear disputes. New Orleans eventually would obtain its own Superior Council.

The Catholic Church provided the other set of laws that applied in New France. New France was under a single Catholic diocese headquartered in Quebec City. The king named and paid the archbishop. Each of the five administrative districts of the Louisiana colony had a bishop. Churches sprang up in or near the forts as small communities grew around the forts. Jesuit and Capuchin priests and missionaries usually riding the circuit performed religious services. The 10 percent tithe ordered in France was hardly ever observed in New France. The priest and missionaries would record all baptisms, weddings, and deaths, usually keeping meticulous records. They mainly concentrated on converting the native Indians to become Catholics. The Indians were considered subjects of the Crown but usually worshipped one God, their chief. All persons of French descent who were born in New France became French citizens.

Unlike the heavy taxes the British Crown imposed in their colony of New England, the French Crown did not levy taxes on the colonists of New France. The colony never produced revenue for the Crown but it did not foster revolt either. The colony had become more of a business venture for well-connected nobility through a monopoly over trade than a money-making enterprise for the Crown. Taxes were not imposed because the Crown wanted to foster trade. The colonists never had to pay the dreaded salt tax (gabelle) as French subjects were forced to pay in the motherland. Salt was an important commodity in both the old and new worlds. Its main use was the preservation of meat.

Chapter Eight

The seigneurial system that developed along the St. Lawrence River and in Canada was never imposed in the Louisiana colony. Although a similar system of long lot division was employed, colonists were granted concessions along the Mississippi River and its tributaries. These land grants (concessions) always had river frontage of two to four leagues in width and sometimes as much as forty to sixty leagues in depth for cultivation and habitation. A concession was an arrangement wherein the Kingdom of France and, later, the Mississippi Company gave to someone the right of use and of ownership of a tract of land in the Louisiana colony. The concession stipulated that the tract would return to the Crown if the tract had not been developed and brought a return within a two-year period. The grantee could not alienate the property until two thirds of the land had been cleared. A concession was free and usually easy to obtain from the Company. The larger and more successful grants went to the nobility, officials of the king's court and persons well connected to John Law. Most of those people never stepped foot in the colony and had no idea where their concession was located. They sent directors and managers to operate their concessions. However, anyone willing to emigrate could have a concession and many concessionaires went to the colony with their workers.

The grant guaranteed the concessionaire a tract of land, however the exact location was to be chosen by a representative of the Mississippi Company upon arrival in the colony.

John Law and his Company directors obtained the prime locations. Bienville received a large concession on the bank of the Mississippi River across from his newly founded Nouvelle Orleans. Concessions usually sprang up around established forts. The colonists needed a place to shelter if the savages went on a warpath. These forts had commanders and royal militias garrisoned there and were paid by the Mississippi Company and/or the king.

The Company provided free passage to the concessionaire and all of his employees and workers on Company ships or ships of the Royal navy. Not wanting the criminals and vagabonds provided by the king, the concessionaires were financially responsible for recruiting and transporting their workers to the port of embarkation. He was also responsible for room and board until they boarded the ship. The concessionaire would send his agents throughout the coastal and farming regions of France to recruit skilled tradesmen, artisans, and laborers who wanted to go to the New World. They recruited barbers, butchers, bakers, and saddle makers; brewers, carpenters, coopers, and candle makers; surgeons, cooks, domestics, and shoemakers; farmers, miners, blacksmiths, and rope makers; engineers, locksmiths, weavers, and tile makers, and even chaplains. These workers contracted with the concessionaire to become engages, usually for a term of three years. These engages were promised food, clothing, and lodging, and usually very meager wages.

Once onboard the Company's ship, the concessionaire, or if he was not going to the colony, his directors and their families, usually ate at the captain's table. The laborers and tradesmen received seaman's rations. The Company allowed and paid for the transport of furniture, kitchenware, clothing, and tools for the tradesmen, however the Company prohibited them from bringing any merchandise for trade. In fact, all goods manufactured or grown in the colony had to be sold to the Company, and all goods not produced or grown by the tradesmen had to be purchased from the Company, a financial impediment that brought impending doom.

The voyage across the Atlantic took the concessionaire and his workers to Biloxi, a poor location for a deep-water port. Anchored off Dauphine Island, the workers and all of their cargo were unloaded on the island and had to be transported by barges and bateaus to the coast about two leagues away. The Company also assumed the obligation of feeding and housing the concessionaire and his workers until they were transported to their concession site. These promises were almost never kept.

Once on shore in the Louisiana colony in Biloxi, the engages soon realized that the harsh conditions on the ship were only a precursor to what lay ahead. The paradise painted by John Law in France was not real. The truth was the colony was more like a hell–swamps infested with alligators and mosquitoes, savage Indians, and usually a lack of food and lodging. Most had to fend for themselves by fishing and hunting for food, or had to rely on the Indians to avoid starvation. They built shanty dwellings with palmetto-thatched roofs to keep out of the weather. If you survived the scurvy, fever, or smallpox on the voyage, you were one of the lucky ones. Many died of disease and starvation in the colony. When your period of engagement ended, the colonist could remain in the colony or passage was paid to return to France.

Francois's heart sank. He knew that to be banished to the Louisiana colony was a sentence of death, even though Pierre still had his life. Francois was not a hating man, but at this moment, he hated Antoine Patin and Minister Dubois more than a man hates the lover of his cheating wife. Francois thought about Marie and knew that the loss of Pierre would break her heart and send her to an early grave.

"What's done is done. Only God can control his fate now. We tried our hardest but came up short. Was there anything more that I could have done?" Francois kept mumbling excuses to Henri as they stood there in a crowd of strangers in the courtroom in Amiens. "I must get out of here and claim my son," said Francois to Henri as he rushed out of the Parlement building with Henri and Landis in tow. His only wish was the opportunity to trade places with Pierre and carry out the sentence himself. The thought of losing his son stirred a feeling of love from the depths of his soul that he had never perfected but finally understood.

His love was so great for Pierre that he asked God to take his life in his son's stead. He had nothing else to live for. He had experienced all that life had to offer. He would willingly give up his future so that Pierre could gain life's rewards. He had so anticipated the day when Pierre would take over his tax farm. He wished for grandchildren from Pierre. He knew those days would never come now.

Out of breath, Henri tried to console Francois when they at last reached the carriage. "This is not the ending but a new beginning for Pierre. He still has his freedom and his life. Let's make the best of it while we still have him here with us," said Henri.

Francois knew Henri was right. Henri was like a brother to Francois and like a second father to Pierre. Pierre used to play at their feet when they first started the tax farm many years ago. Francois graciously accepted Henri's advice and decided to make the next two months as joyous an occasion as possible for Pierre. Francois's only concern now was to get Pierre back to his mother.

Landis was familiar with the city of Amiens as he had been there on a number of occasions with Henri and Francois. He drove the carriage directly to the royal prison. Francois disembarked and entered the prison only to reappear a short time later without Pierre. Henri and Landis were waiting near the carriage.

"God help us. They say that Pierre will not be available for release until the morning. Looks like we will be in Amiens another night," said Francois.

"Why don't we get something to eat and then go over to the royal bank to see what we can get for our banknotes from Arnaud," suggested Henri.

They arrived at the royal bank of Amiens, this time with the bag full of banknotes they received from the sale of their shares in the Mississippi Company. The manager of the bank, Mr. Arnaud, welcomed them back from their trip to Paris.

"Glad to see you again. I hope your trip to Paris was successful," said Arnaud as Henri and Francois walked into his office.

"We sold our two hundred shares at 12,500 livres per share. We have two million five hundred livres of banknotes in this satchel, which we would like to exchange for silver and gold coins. The better news is Pierre is to be released tomorrow; the bad news is the magistrate sentenced him to the Louisiana colony for life," said Francois nearly in tears.

"I am so sorry to hear that," said Arnaud. "In a way, Pierre may be better off than all of us. I am afraid there is a financial storm brewing on the near horizon here in France. John Law keeps changing the bank rules. First, he says banknotes can be exchanged for silver, and then he says we cannot exchange them for silver. He has been fiddling with the exchange rate at which we can convert banknotes to silver. To make matters worse, he has been repurchasing shares in the Mississippi Company with new banknotes resulting in a huge increase in outstanding notes floating around. The repurchases tend to keep demand for the stock high and thus it artificially raises the price. Too many banknotes chasing too few goods make prices go up. There is word that he is about to start devaluing both the price of the shares and the exchange rate on the banknotes."

"Emily told us as much. You know her husband, Leon, works for the royal bank in Paris," said Henri.

"Do you have sufficient coinage on hand to cash in our notes?" asked Francois.

"Are you jesting? I can cash some of them in for you at parity. Just last week I was giving one silver livre for one-and-a-half banknote of livre. Today, it's at one livre to five banknotes. I know I do not have enough coins on hand to exchange all of your notes. Our coinage supply has been shrinking. How about fifty thousand in silver and gold coins? You are depleting my reserves to the bare bones," said Arnaud.

"That would be wonderful," said Henri. "I guess we will hold on to the remainder of our banknotes and spend them as fast as we can."

"You have been a true friend to us throughout the years, Arnaud," said Francois. "I will always appreciate your good faith dealings with us. Can we leave the coins and banknotes here until tomorrow, after we retrieve Pierre? I don't want to carry around that sum of money."

The next morning, Francois was up early again, in anticipation of the release of Pierre. The day he had longed for had finally arrived. He was to get his son back, even if it was only for a couple of months. At least he was alive and free. He had arranged a hot bath for Pierre at the inn and bought him a new change of clothes from a local seamstress. Francois sent Landis to bring the carriage around to the front of the inn to load their few belongings and their newly acquired guest. They were off early to the royal prison to rescue Pierre from his misery. Francois and Henri went inside. The paper work was unexpectedly in order and Pierre was released to Francois's custody for a small sum in bail.

"You look awful," said Henri to Pierre as a guard brought him into the front office.

"I feel awful," said Pierre.

"Your father has arranged for you a bath at the Boor's Nest Inn and bought you a new change of clothes," said Henri.

"I so appreciate all you and Father have done for me. I do not know how much longer I could have lasted in this filthy place. The New World cannot be as bad as this," said Pierre.

"You smell like dead, rotting animals. Let's be off," said Francois. "Henri will stay with you at the inn while I take care of some business at the royal bank."

Pierre walked out the door of the prison with Francois and Henri in tow hoping to never see a place like that again. The warmth of the sun on Pierre's face helped brighten up his spirits. His dark damp cell was now only a horrible reminder of the disgrace of his short confinement. Yet, he did gain a greater appreciation for his freedom, and the whole ordeal made him realize the importance of always doing the right thing at all times. Wrong decisions often brought grave consequences. He looked at Landis sitting in the driver's seat of the carriage and smiled as he greeted him with a faint tear puddling in the corner of his eye. He longed to see Simone and his mother.

Landis rushed Pierre and Henri to the Boar's Nest Inn. Waiting for Pierre, in a room off the front desk in the lobby, was a large wooden tub. The tub was filled with hot water as Pierre removed his dirty, smelly clothes—the same clothes he had been wearing for over a week now. The attendant provided Pierre with a bar of lye soap made with olive oil and lavender in the south of France. His new set of clothing was set on a chair in the room, and the attendant and Henri exited. Pierre climbed in, relaxed, and scrubbed the grime as if washing away a layer of his life he did not want to remember.

While Pierre was reclaiming his pride in life, Francois and Landis proceeded to the royal bank to retrieve the spoils of their prior life. In a way, Pierre's misfortune became a fortunate event for Henri and Francois. But for Pierre's incarceration, they would not have been informed of the necessity of selling their stock in the Mississippi Company or of its impending doom. A devaluation of the banknotes and stock before the sale would have cost them most of their life savings. Landis loaded the strong box of the carriage until it was overflowing, at one point dropping silver coins everywhere and being scolded by Francois. He managed to get them all to fit after filling their pockets with the excess. They rushed back to the inn, picked up Henri and Pierre, and headed for home.

"You finally look and smell like a gentleman again," Francois said to his son as they settled in for their long carriage ride to Maintenay.

"Your father and I have been discussing a party in your honor to celebrate your release and your new start in life. What do you think, Pierre?" asked Henri.

"I am truly ashamed about the whole ordeal," said Pierre. "But it would be nice to see Emily before my departure. Yes, a party would be good. We can invite Simone and her family, you and your family, Henri, and Father's employees at the company."

"We can have the party at the house," said Francois. "I guess I will have to befriend Simone, even though you know I never did approve of your relationship. I should never have had her family start farming our land. You probably would not be in this state of affairs if not for her."

"Father, I plan to marry Simone if she will come with me to the New World."

Francois was overcome with emotion. He had so wanted a better life for Pierre—a clergyman's daughter for a wife, taking over the tax farm, maybe even becoming a nobleman. He never approved of their relationship because he knew Pierre deserved more than an uneducated peasant girl as a wife. Now this peasant girl was the cause of losing Pierre forever. She brought only misery and misfortune into Pierre's life. Francois's dislike of her soon turned into hatred and disgust. Francois was determined to intervene at last. He thought long and hard during the remainder of his trip home.

Landis was the most excited about getting home, even more than Pierre. As he rounded the last curve on the approach to Francois's house, he could see in the distance a faint glow of a candle burning from the front room window. He had been traveling for some time since the sun went down. He was tired, hot, and dirty from all the dust that the bumpy, dirt roads managed to produce. It must have been ten or eleven at night, he thought, as he pulled up to the spot he and his companions had left several days before.

Pierre was the first to get out of the carriage, and he hurriedly made his way to the front door to see his mother. The door opened as he got there.

"Pierre," said Marie as she reached forward to steal a big hug and give him a kiss.

"Oh, mother, it is so good to be home and see you," said Pierre as he hugged and kissed her in return. "They are sending me to the Louisiana colony for my punishment. I sail in less than two months."

"What? I don't believe you. This cannot be so," said Marie with a gasp.

"You heard right," said Francois as he approached from the carriage. "That was the best we could do for his release."

"That cannot be so," Marie said again. She began to sob and turned and went into the house.

Pierre followed her in. "Hello, Henrietta," said Pierre to their cook and maid as he intersected her heading to the kitchen.

"Let's see what we can find for four hungry fellows," said Henrietta as she greeted Pierre with a hug and kiss. "I think I might have some ham and leftover biscuits."

By this time, Joseph, the groundskeeper and manager of the farm, had taken the horses and carriage and placed them in the barn. After being paid with several silver coins, Landis left for home on his horse. Henri and Francois made their way into the house and entered the kitchen where Pierre had begun to eat his meal. It was his first good meal in a week. Everyone was in a somber mood. Marie's sadness had spread to Pierre and Henrietta.

"Marie, you have to look on the positive side. Pierre could have been imprisoned for several years or he could have even been hanged. This is a much better alternative. He will be an engage for three years and can come home to France after his tour of duty is over," said Henri as he tried to console Marie with a lie. They had decided not to tell her that Pierre was going over as a convict for life. He and Francois knew that a sentence as a prison laborer was much harsher than becoming an engage. Francois could only stare at the candle burning on the table.

"I am sure my wife has been worried. I must head home myself. We will settle up on the stock sale in a day or two," said Henri as he walked out of the kitchen and toward the front door. "Good night, all."

"Thanks for the company and the encouragement, good friend. See you soon," said Francois as he walked Henri to the door. "I will explain it all to Marie in the morning. I think I need a good night's rest first."

Chapter Nine

The planting season had begun. It was May 1, 1720, only a week or so after Pierre's release. The sweet smell of freshly turned ground wafted in the evening air as the picturesque redness in the western sky delighted the guests. Everyone on the invitation list for Pierre's party had arrived, with the exception of Nicholas who always seemed to be late for everything. Emily and Leon had come the night before from Paris. Their invitation had been sent by post as soon as Francois had returned from Paris. Everyone else's invitation had been hand delivered.

Henri and his wife had been there since early afternoon to help prepare for the party. Landis, Joseph, and Henrietta were busy preparing the food, with Landis taking care of the *cochon de lait*. The pig was split down the breast bone and opened up so that two medal rods, one through the top shoulders and one through the rump roasts, conveniently splayed the pig for roasting. The pig was hung close to a confined fire with direct heat. Landis had to continually tug the string tied to the hanging pig so the pig would slowly swing around and around to cook evenly. Francois opened a cask of brandy for the guests. Hardly ever getting a chance to drink such a fine refreshment, Landis partook one too many and was all but drunk by the time supper was ready. He almost burnt the pig.

Simone and her mother and father, Mr. and Mrs. Beniot, had arrived, as had the employees of the tax farm. Even surrounding neighbors made an appearance; the word of Pierre's fate had gotten around the small town of Maintenay. Everyone seemed to be in a festive mood, but it was somewhat awkward attending a *bon voyage* party for someone convicted of robbery and sentenced to the New World. However, the guests were mostly family and close friends. All understood the need to encourage Pierre.

"The party seems to be going well. Pierre seems to be in high spirits, although I heard him talking to his mother again about asking for Simone's hand in marriage," said Henri to Francois as they milled around the front lawn.

"Yes, that still bothers me. Henri, I have come up with a plan to aid Pierre, and I want your considered opinion. I never told you this, but Simone did acquire more than Antione Patin's tax receipts on the night of the robbery. She acquired two sets of books. One set of books notates the actual tax receipts he collects, and the other set are the ones he uses for the accounting to the Crown. He has been skimming tax receipts and sharing them with Minister Guillaume Dubois. Pierre has seen the books and verified as much."

"That no account crook!" shouted Henri.

"I'm sorry I did not tell you this other fact, either. Dubois demanded both sets of books within two weeks when I met with him in Paris. He may take our tax farm or worse. This is my plan: I propose to send Landis with a letter to Dubois promising to relinquish the books on the condition that Pierre be sent to the Louisiana colony as an employee of the Mississippi Company or as a concessionaire and not as a prison laborer for the Company. I will also get a pledge from him not to interfere with our tax farm. If he does not accept these conditions, I will reveal his scheme to John Law and the regent and he will suffer the consequences as we may. He will go to the guillotine for stealing from the Crown, and I will ask as much. What have you to say about my proposal?" asked Francois.

"I think it is a great plan. We have nothing to lose. But what if Dubois refuses? Or worse yet, what if Dubois agrees, we turn over the books and then he reneges on the deal?" asked Henri.

"We must demand a response from Minister Dubois in writing and make sure he understands that he will not get the books until we have a commitment for Pierre in writing. We shall draft the letter in the morning and send Landis to Paris immediately. Agreed?"

"Agreed," said Henri.

"Good evening, Monsieur Beniot," said Francois to Simone's father as they came upon him. "How is the planting coming along?"

"Very well, sir. Hope to make a good crop of barley and wheat this year. We just need some good rains," said Mr. Beniot.

"Pierre has been talking about marriage to your daughter. What do you think of such talk?" asked Francois.

"I heard as much. I am not so tendin to the idea. She is real young and Mrs. Beniot don't look favorable on her going to the New World with all those savages and such. We prone not to lose an extra hand in the field," said Mr. Beniot.

"I am of the same opinion," said Francois. "I will make it a point to speak with Mrs. Beniot tonight."

"We can't thank you enough, Monsieur Mayeux, for not gettin Simone in trouble by tellin about her effort in this wrongdoin. And we are so obliged for the chance to farm your land," said Mr. Beniot.

"You don't know how thankful I am for you and your family, Monsieur Beniot," said Francois with a feigned smile on his face.

"There is Simone now. I must have a word with her. Excuse me, Monsieur Beniot," said Francois. He noticed Simone was alone in the yard. He hurried toward her.

"Simone," shouted Francois. "May I speak with you?"

Simone looked nervous as Francois approached her.

"Pierre tells me that you have a set of books that you acquired in your criminal caper against Antoine Patin. Is that correct?" asked Francois.

"Yes, I have them hidden in a hole in the ground."

"Simone, you know I do not approve of your relationship with Pierre. But I have a proposition to make you, for Pierre's sake. I will pay you one thousand livres for those books if you agree that you will not go to the New World with Pierre."

"But he and I was thinkin bout gettin married," said Simone.

"Yes, that means the marriage is off, and Pierre will go to the New World alone. However, the most important part of our agreement is that you cannot tell anyone about it, not even Pierre. If you break your promise, you may force me to tell the royal guard about your involvement in the crime against Antoine Patin. And I may take away your father's farming privileges on my land. We do not want that to happen, do we? If Pierre asks to see the books, tell him you threw them away. Do we have a deal?"

"I have such feelins for Pierre, but a thousand livres would help our family. My mother wasn't keen on me goin to the New World noways. Pierre was sure set on gettin married though. This will break his heart. But if you say it is for Pierre's sake, I will agree," said Simone.

Francois was ashamed at the depths to which one could sink in a time of crisis. He had always been a good and honest man in his fidelity to his wife and in his business dealings. The poor girl did not know what she possessed. She possessed Pierre's life in her hands. She would not have understood it anyway. Her only exposure to the written word was the missal at the Catholic Mass and that was in Latin. Francois knew those were not legitimate excuses. God would understand though. Francois did it all for his son.

The party went on well into the night. Everyone had their fill of food and drink. Landis managed to salvage most of the roasted pig. Everyone gave their well wishes to Pierre, except his brother Nicholas who commented in front of some of the guests that Pierre would have a difficult time as a laborer in the Louisiana colony since he never did a lick of manual labor in his life. Finally, everyone had gone home. Emily, Leon, Francois, and Marie went to bed, as had Henrietta and Joseph. Only one guest remained.

"Pierre, I can not marry you," said Simone as they sat on the front porch and were being serenaded by the crickets. The light of the full moon showed the seriousness of Simone's countenance.

"You are all I thought about while in prison. I love you, Simone. How can you say you will not marry me?" asked Pierre.

"I love you too, Pierre, and I am sorry I got you into this mess, but I was not plannin on going to the New World. Besides, my mother and father need me here, on the farm," said Simone.

"Well, let's go to Italy. I don't want to go to the Louisiana colony, either. We can elope and live on the run in Europe."

"They will find us, Pierre," said Simone.

"You keep finding excuses. You must not love me as much as I love you. Come on, let's go to the barn," said Pierre. He reached over and kissed her. She returned the affection and followed him, hand in hand, as he pulled her from the porch. "We have not had sex for over a month."

Simone undressed Pierre, and Pierre undressed Simone. Their bodies came together with such passion, as if they were two lovers who had been separated for years. The hay made a comfortable bed to ignite their infatuation. After making love for what seemed like hours, they laid there naked and nearly half asleep.

"I will go to the New World with or without you. I cannot further jeopardize Father's tax farm. I will do my time of servitude and come back to France for you," whispered Pierre as they dozed off to sleep.

The spring turned into early summer. Fields of green wheat and barley were planted and strove to reach the sun. Gardens of potato, maize, and tomato plants, only recently introduced into Europe from the New World, were thriving. Life had gotten back to a semblance of order for the Mayeux family. Francois acquired the two sets of books from Simone after paying her the agreed upon amount of one thousand livres. Pierre had somehow taken to the idea of going to the New World as a new adventure. Landis was dispatched to Paris with the letter to Minister Dubois.

In the letter, Francois threatened to turn over the books to the regent if Francois did not receive a letter from the regent commuting Pierre's sentence, and a letter from John Law making Pierre an employee of the Mississippi Company or a concessionaire. Landis was ordered to wait in Paris for a response from Minister Dubois. The set of books were not sent with Landis. Francois had to retain some bargaining power.

Pierre had been mentally preparing for his trip, for such a trip takes mental as well as physical fortitude. He had been reading all published works that he could get his hands on about the Louisiana colony and the Mississippi Company. Pierre discovered that the regent had put an end to deportation of criminals to the Louisiana colony by edict of the king on May 9, 1720. He quickly discovered that things were changing in both France and the New World.

"We should leave for La Rochelle at least a week before the sailing date of June tenth," said Pierre to Francois. They discussed his departure while taking account of the tax receipts for the day at the office.

"You are probably right. La Rochelle is twice the distance from here to Paris. It will take three good days by carriage. The trip will be a hard ride for your mother, assuming she will make the trip," said Francois.

"Mother, not making the trip? Don't be foolish. Anyway, I would like to see Emily and Leon again before I go. We can leave early to make a stop in Paris," said Pierre.

"You are probably right," said Francois. "We are going to miss you, Pierre," said Francois. He tried to hold back his tears. "You know your mother and I love you, even though I never seem to get around to telling you that."

"I love you too, Father, and I will miss you," said Pierre. He reached out to give Francois a hug. He felt awkward as he had never hugged his father and this was the first time he'd told his father he loved him. "From what I have read, living in the colony will not be easy."

"No, it will not be, especially working as a convict laborer. I am going to send you with as much silver as you can lug. I hope it will carry you over in the tough times. I will try to send you livres every chance I get. I am just not sure how," said Francois.

"We should probably leave by June fourth. That's only three days away," said Pierre. "I guess I will bring my small chest for my belongings."

"I will get Landis to drive us. He just returned from Paris with some good news. I did not tell you this before today for fear of getting your hopes up. I got a hold of those books belonging to Antoine Patin and discovered, as you assumed, that he is skimming tax collections. He is conspiring with Minister Dubois in the scheme. I confirmed as much when I approached Dubois for your release. I sent Landis with a letter to Minister Dubois to exchange the books for your service as an employee of the Mississippi Company instead of a convict laborer. Dubois has agreed! I have been waiting for Dubois's rider who will pick up the books and deliver a letter from John Law confirming your employment or even a concession. I am worried now that your day of departure is near with still no word from Dubois."

"Father that gives me so much pleasure and gratitude that you would do such a thing, exposing your business for me. Thank you so much. It means a great deal to me," said Pierre. He hugged his father again. Displays of affection became easier.

The morning of June fourth arrived with no word from Minister Dubois. Pierre made all the rounds to say goodbye the week prior: Henri and his family, Simone and her family, his relatives and friends, and the employees of the tax farm.

Landis was late again on the scheduled day of departure. The sun was already a few degrees above the horizon. It was a clear summer morning. The birds were chirping as the dew melted from the night before. The smell of smoke from the hearth fire inside the Mayeux home mixed with the morning fog and drifted over the slow rolling hills of Maintenay. Nicholas had stayed over the night before, and Pierre expected Simone at any moment to say her final goodbyes. Everyone had just finished the breakfast that Henrietta prepared of biscuits and ham with fresh apples, pears, peaches, and figs from the orchard. Joseph pulled the carriage under the carriage porch at the side door of the house, off the kitchen. Francois requested four horses for the carriage and they were harnessed and waiting.

"Someone is knocking at the front door. Can you answer it, Henrietta?" asked Marie as she scurried around the kitchen in a nervous mess.

She normally did not make these long trips, especially a trip to send off her son to a new and distant land. The thought was making her jump around the kitchen like a chicken with its head cut off. "Who is it?" she asked with nervous anticipation as if a visitor would calm her nerves.

"It's Simone," responded Henrietta.

"Well, have her to come in. Where is Pierre?" shouted Marie.

"Hello, Simone," said Nicholas as he came down the stairs into the foyer. "I think Pierre is helping Joseph load the carriage at the side entrance. Now that Pierre is gone, maybe you and I can start an affair."

"I wouldn't count on it," said Simone. She hurriedly went to the kitchen to meet Pierre outside.

"Simone, I am so glad you made it. I was beginning to think you would not come," said Pierre as he gave her a kiss and held her in his arms. "This may be the last time I see you in a very long while."

"I know. When you write home, please write to me, too. I'll get your mother to read the letters," said Simone.

"Let's get going. Landis is finally here," said Francois, who had retrieved the set of books and a large quantity of silver coinage from his secret hiding place and placed them in the strong box of the carriage.

Everyone gathered around Pierre to say their last goodbyes and each in turn gave him a hug. Nicholas stood in the doorway of the kitchen and waved. "Maybe I'll come see you in the Louisiana colony."

"That would be great," said Pierre as he walked up to his big brother and shook his hand. With everyone in the carriage waiting, Pierre climbed the steps waving with tears in his eyes and closed the door. Landis cracked the whip and they were off to Amiens, then Paris, and then on to the port at La Rochelle.

By edict of the king on May 22, 1720, John Law devalued the price per share of the Mississippi Company from nine thousand to five thousand livres and all of the royal banknotes by one half. Everyone wanted to sell their stock in the Mississippi Company. But hardly anyone was buying. The price plummeted. The run on banks continued as investors demanded coinage in exchange for their banknotes. Riots ensued. People were trampled to death as they lined up at banks to make withdrawals. On May 27, 1720, the edict was reversed and the banknotes were restored to their previous value. However, the damage had been done. Inflation was running at a monthly rate of over 20 percent. The whole of France lost confidence in the monetary system and the Mississippi Company. On May 28, 1720, John Law was dismissed from the Company and placed under house arrest. However, within days, he was released and resumed his seat as Minister of Finance. The regent realized that only John Law knew enough about the monetary system to save it. Only he could save from bankruptcy the monster that he had created.

The Louisiana colony suffered because of the financial troubles in France. John Law had been selling established plantations in the colony for three thousand livres per square league to nobility and rich merchants. The noble classes who made these purchases never went to the colony, however, thus the plantations lacked direct supervision and financial support. Mineral resources did not exist, so the colonists attempted agriculture. Indigo and tobacco were their main cash crops. Lumber from the abundant forests proved profitable, as Europe had by this time become deforested. The colony suffered from lack of laborers, so they imported slaves.

There was no financial benefit to the plantation owners because they bought everything from the Company and sold everything to the Company. The Europeans who did come to the colony were financiers or merchants. Some were tailors, butchers, carpenters, barbers, sailors, militia, coopers, and even criminals, but most did not want to do the manual labor of clearing the land, planting and harvesting the crops, and building roads and levees–the real work that grew a colony. Most were employees or engages of the Company. French soldiers were sent on occasion to help quell Indian revolts but most returned after their term of engagement expired. Slaves were being imported but not in sufficient numbers to satisfy the needs of the owners of the land grants. Commandant General Bienville's continued pleas to discontinue the importation of criminals were finally recognized. The criminals and vagabonds were burdens on the Company and the colony, as they could never get any work out of them. Serious immigration into the colony did not begin until 1718 and lasted until about 1721. Nearly six thousand Europeans found their ancestors' names on passenger lists and made the long voyage from La Rochelle, Le Havre, Cherbourg, Brest, Lorient, and other French ports. Many died of sickness or disease on the voyage to the colony, which could take two to four months depending on the weather and time of year.

John Law established for himself a land grant at the Arkansas post consisting of four leagues square. He sent a company of dragoons, one-and-a-half-million livres worth of merchandise and fifteen hundred male German engages to work the land. Militia, paid by the company, staffed the forts and each fort had a commandant. The forts had warehouses from which the colonists bought and sold their produce and commodities at Company rates. The Mississippi Company in New Orleans sold slaves. However, the colonists often sold slaves and other merchandise among themselves, which was against the law. Merchandise of the Company was sold in New Orleans at a 50 percent profit on the original cost in France; at the Natchez post at a 75 percent profit; and at the Arkansas Post at a 100 percent profit. In 1721, slaves sold for six hundred sixty livres per person; rice, twelve livres per barrel; wine, twenty-six livres per cask; brandy, one hundred twenty livres per cask. Muskets, powder, and shot were also prized commodities.

Chapter Ten

La Rochelle was a beautiful and thriving city on the coast of France. The city surrounded a deep-water harbor that accommodated trade from around the Old and New Worlds. It was once a walled city surrounded by a ten-foot stone wall made from stone cut from nearby quarries. Two tall harbor towers made of stone guarded the entrance from the sea. During the mid-1500s, Protestants began to occupy the city as Calvinism became firmly established. This led to religious wars with the Catholic ruling nobility. In the 1620s, the Huguenots began to openly challenge the authority of King Louis XIII. His chief minister, Cardinal Richelieu, decided to quell the revolt in La Rochelle and placed the city under siege for nearly a year and a half. The Huguenots fiercely resisted. Nearly starved and unable to break the siege, they surrendered the city. Catholicism became the official religion of the city again. The Huguenots finally abandoned the city for the New World during the 1680s under the reign of King Louis XIV, the Sun King. LaSalle had departed from La Rochelle on his ill-fated trip to find the mouth of the Mississippi by way of the Gulf of Mexico. By 1720, the city was once again a thriving trading port, handling the slave trade from Africa, the fur trade from Canada, and the sugar and coffee trade from the Caribbean. The merchant class formed a bustling community around the shipping business. There were ship builders, sail makers, barrel makers, traders, and waggoneers. The various tradesmen worked from dawn to dusk.

❧

The carriage ride was long, bumpy, hot, and dusty—not unusual for travel on the dirt roads of France in the summertime. Landis got them to Amiens by early evening so they stopped at the Boor's Nest for the night. They left Amiens before sunup the next morning and reached Paris early that evening. Francois had instructed Landis to go directly to Emily's house, even though she was not expecting them. They arrived to a charming cottage just across the Seine outside of the old walls of the formerly fortified city.

"Pierre!" shouted Emily as she responded to a knock at her door. "What are you doing here?"

"I came to say my final goodbye," said Pierre to his big sister. She gave him an embrace. "Mother and Father are here with me. I think father is sending Landis off to the inn for the night."

"Come in and have a seat with Leon. I am sure you are tired of traveling. What can I get you to drink?" asked Emily.

"My journey has only just begun. I understand that it can take two to three months to cross the ocean. I don't know if I want to go," said Pierre. He requested anything that might satisfy his thirst.

"Mother and Father, come in. What an unexpected surprise. I did not realize that Pierre would be leaving this early," said Emily as Marie and Francois entered the vestibule.

"We are a little early because I have to attend to some business in Paris tomorrow," said Francois. "Hello, Leon. Do you know Minister Dubois or John Law?"

"No, I have only seen them in passing. I have never met them personally. What is this all about?" asked Leon.

"Just unfinished business. I met Dubois once and I suspect I shall meet him again in the morning. Then we are off to La Rochelle. We want to get there a day or two early. Have you ever been to La Rochelle, Leon?" asked Francois, starting a casual conversation with him to divert his attention from any pretense about the scheme he had concocted. Leon took the hint. Francois did not want to get

Leon and his daughter involved in any way with those depraved, filthy scoundrels in Paris.

Emily was a cordial hostess. She served her three guests wine and supper while Leon told them of the hysteria gripping Paris and the dire state of affairs with the financial system of France and the Mississippi Company, and the near certain possibility of a financial crash. He had heard Law was relieved of his duties as Minister of Finance and had been placed under house arrest, again. Pierre wondered about the fate of the Louisiana Colony and what he was about to get himself into. After a long visit, they all retired for the evening.

Landis was at the cottage early the next morning. Apparently, he got some sleep and did not attempt to find Lancelot the night before . The long carriage ride the previous two days had taken its toll and he knew he had at least two more days of riding. He and Francois left for the Palais-Royal immediately to find Minister Dubois. The ride into the city became familiar as they crossed the Pont Neuf and passed Notre Dame Cathedral. Upon their arrival at the Palais-Royal, Francois discovered, to his disappointment, that the minister would not be able to see him. He was preoccupied with matters of the kingdom. Francois was instructed by a courtier to leave correspondence relaying his intentions and place of abode and the minister would send a reply. Thereupon, Francois wrote the minister a letter.

Dear Minister Dubois: 6th June 1720

I have in my possession the articles that you desire. I have not yet received the object of my desire. My son, Pierre Mayeux, and I are leaving for La Rochelle on this very day to fulfill the execution of his sentence. Please have the letter from John Law regarding the service of my son with the Mississippi Company in my possession before the morning of June 10 or you will have hell to pay. We will be staying at the Pontchartrain Inn in La Rochelle.

Signed,

Francois Mayeux

Francois and Landis hurried back to Emily's home and Francois informed Pierre of the dire news. Francois and Pierre decided to leave for La Rochelle immediately and to break up the carriage ride there into two days, for Marie's sake. They passed through the city of Orleans and stopped in the city of Tours for the night. They arrived in La Rochelle in the early morning hours of June eighth and obtained lodging at the Pontchartrain Inn. A letter from Minister Dubois had not preceded them.

"I think I will take a walk to the pier to see if I can find the *La Profond*," said Pierre to his father as they were finishing a late breakfast at a tavern next to the inn.

"If you wait until I finish, I'll come with you," said Francois.

"No, I think I will go alone." The bright mid-morning sun's rays filled the town. All of the hustle and bustle was a constant distraction for Pierre. He walked down the street from the tavern, but he had to ask directions to the harbor. It was only a few blocks. Wonderful smells emanated from the various store fronts. He walked past a baker's shop and a boucherie with hanging meats, a tannery and a tailor's shop. He walked past a huge stone building, three stories tall and four blocks long, used to make hundreds of leagues of rope. Store fronts of fresh fruit and vegetables and seafood of all sorts, mainly fish, lined one street. The salty air told him he was close to the harbor. As he rounded a corner, he came upon a magnificent scene–a large harbor filled with ships of all sizes, including tall sailing ships. All of this activity somehow excited Pierre. He knew he was soon going to be, in some way, and whether he liked it or not, starting a new life.

His eyes were immediately drawn to one huge ship that had its sails set and was underway, struggling mightily with the wind. Pierre asked around but could not find the *La Profond*. Everyone seemed to be too busy loading or unloading goods, inspecting cargo or hauling it to and from the wharf in horse-drawn wagons. He decided to head back to the tavern.

After a few blocks down a cobbled street, he came upon a shoemaker's shop. Deciding a new pair of shoes for his trip would be a good idea, he entered and saw a young cobbler at work behind the counter. The smell of tanned leather permeated the room. Various tools hung on the wall and lay on the workbench. The cobbler was busy at work stitching a sole on a shoe.

"May I help you?" asked the cobbler.

"I need a pair of good leather work boots," said Pierre.

"Let me take some measurements. Are you a new tradesman here in La Rochelle?" asked the cobbler as he came around the counter to greet Pierre.

"No, I will be a passenger on the *La Profond* heading for the Louisiana colony," responded Pierre, ashamed at letting him know that he would be traveling there as a prisoner of the Crown.

"God save the king. I will be a passenger on the *La Profond* myself. My master has secured me a position with the Mississippi Company as a shoemaker and tailor. We sail in only two days."

"I know," said Pierre.

"I'll get right on these boots and you can come by tomorrow afternoon. They will be ready," said the cobbler.

"My name is Pierre Mayeux. What's yours?" asked Pierre as he extended his hand in greeting.

"Adrien LeBeau, at your service."

"Well, Adrien LeBeau, it is my pleasure meeting you. I will be here tomorrow afternoon for the boots. Maybe we can take a tour of the harbor and find the *La Profond*," said Pierre.

"Sure, I know exactly where she is anchored," said Adrien.

Pierre returned to the tavern excited with anticipation to tell his parents of his newfound friend. He wondered if providence had brought them together. He was happy and relieved that he would not be getting on the ship alone. At least now he had a companion on the voyage to the New World. Pierre knew that he would have to tell Adrien about his reason for traveling to the Louisiana colony. He just wondered when and how he would do it. He was ashamed because he was of the bourgeoisie. Saddled with this kind of future was barbaric to him. Pride raised its repulsive reaction for which shame could not succumb or sedate.

Francois and Marie were delighted with the news that Pierre happened upon someone sailing on the *La Profond*. Francois insisted that he meet Adrien the next morning. The morning of June ninth arrived and yet there was still no letter from Minister Dubois. But circumstances seemed to have shifted in Pierre's favor. The growing excitement of the voyage masked the unpleasant feeling surrounding the whole circumstance.

"I am anxious to meet Adrien," said Francois as he and Pierre walked to the shoemaker's shop after breakfast.

"He seems to be an interesting young man. I do not know much about him. Maybe we should have him as our guest for dinner, a sort of bon voyage party," said Pierre to his father as they reached the entrance of the shop. "I see Adrien is in."

"Good morning, Pierre; good to see you again, my friend. I have those boots almost ready for you. I worked on them all day yesterday afternoon and into the night," said Adrien.

"Adrien, I would like you to meet my father, Monsieur Francois Mayeux. Father, Adrien LeBeau," said Pierre.

"Very nice to meet you, Adrien. I understand you will be a passenger on the *La Profond*," said Francois.

"Yes, my master here at the shop paid thirty livres for my passage. A recruiter came by looking for cobblers and tailors to work on a concession. I hope to be employed with the Mississippi Company when we get there," said Adrien. "Here, Pierre, try on your boots. They are my gift to you."

"I'll try them on later. Let's take a look at our ship. I have never been on one. Have you?" asked Pierre.

"Oh yes, plenty of times. Come on. I will show you fellows around. We can see if a passenger list is posted yet," said Adrien as he hollered to the shop owner in the back, informing him that he was leaving for a few minutes.

"What do you know about the ship?" asked Francois as Adrien led them to the harbor.

"She is a king's vessel, a man-of-war of fifty guns–*de vaisseaux La Profond*. She served in Canada under Iberville and saw action during The War of the Spanish Succession. She is at least twenty-five years old. She must be a hallowed ship to have survived for so long and still not buried in the deep. She will be under the command of Monsieur Du Guermuer De Pemanech," said Adrien.

"I guess I was lucky never to have fought in any of King Louis XIV's wars," said Francois as they made their way to the wharf. "I did my duty to help finance them, though."

"There she is, anchored in the harbor. She has been undergoing careening for the last month. They just finished loading her with cargo and supplies yesterday. She is waiting for us," said Adrien with a smile.

"She is a majestic ship," said Francois.

"I see the crew are already onboard working," said Pierre.

"Yes, they were paid one quarter of their wages when they boarded several days ago. They have been preparing the sails, arranging the cargo, stocking the galley and storehouses," said Adrien.

"How do you know so much about sailing?" asked Pierre.

"I have made lots of voyages across the Atlantic. Let's check the passenger list. It should be posted on the wharf," said Adrien.

Workmen and tradesmen were busy careening another ship. Pierre had to watch his step so as not to get run over by dock workers moving buckets, barrels, and bales. Merchants were out inspecting goods and making deals. Pierre saw an abundance of goods on the docks: casks of wine and brandy, salt, tobacco, sugar, flour, coffee, salted meats including pork, manufactured goods such as textiles and luxury items. Chickens were in coops. Cattle and pigs were in pens–future meals for a captain's table.

After some searching, Adrien found the passenger list tacked to a post under a board that kept it out of the weather somewhat. Pierre wondered to himself about the role Adrien played in the French fleet. He seemed to have considerable knowledge of ships and lots of sailing experience.

"Here's your name–Pierre Mayeux. Convict?" asked Adrien with a dazed look of confusion on his face.

"Yes, I was going to tell you but I didn't know when or how. Come have supper with us tonight at the tavern next to Pontchartrain Inn. I'll tell you the whole story."

"I surely will," said Adrien. He was not at all concerned that his traveling partner was a criminal. Adrien had had his share of bouts with the law. Anyway, the thought of a good meal before the voyage was just fine by him. "Here's my name listed as a cobbler/tailor from La Rochelle, France, but my age is wrong. I am twenty-two not twenty-five."

"These lists are not terribly accurate. I am not from Amiens," said Pierre.

"It looks like we will be transporting troops for the Royal Army–some twenty-five to thirty of them by my count. Pierre Borgne, age twenty-six, of Troyes in Champagne, 5', black hair, dyer; Antoine LaRoche, age twenty, of Macon, 5', auburn hair, weaver; Pierre Vaugois, age eighteen, of Fennes in Bretagne, 4'4", black hair, barber of wig-maker; Louis Menard, age thirty-five, of Longueville in Poitou, 4' 10", black hair, butcher; Poussine, age fourteen; Thibault, age sixteen," continued Adrien as Pierre chimed in.

"Here are the employees of the Dartaguiette Concession, about thirty in all. There are two Jesuit missionaries and a few representatives from the Company. A majority of the passengers are engages for John Law's concession, about one hundred eighty or so. It seems I am listed with the convicts and vagabonds, about ten of us," said Pierre.

"Yes, you will be eating seamen rations with me. Passage on the king's vessel is free for members of the court, Company employees, soldiers, and missionaries and nuns. Others can pay thirty livres for passage with crew rations. There are a few passengers paying the one-hundred-fifty-livre price to eat at the captain's table. They may be merchants that have business in the Louisiana colony. I'd say we will have about two hundred fifty passengers onboard," said Adrien.

"Only a few are making the crossing on their own free will," said Pierre. "Most are being encouraged–the troops by the king, Company employees by John Law, criminals and vagabonds by the magistrates, engages by the concessionaires and missionaries of God," said Pierre.

"People are not lining up to go to the Louisiana colony, are they?" quipped Francois. "How many crew members are on the ship, Adrien?"

"About two hundred fifty to three hundred for a ship of fifty guns during war time, sir. We might have one hundred for this voyage," said Adrien. "I need to get back to the shop."

"Will we see you at six o'clock for supper?" asked Pierre.

"I'll be there, and I will bring your shoes," said Adrien.

The French sailing fleet consisted of two types of vessels: the king's vessels and the merchant marine. The king used his vessels for war and transport of troops. His ships included the men-of-war, frigates, flutes, corvettes, and barges. The merchant marine had similar ships but they were privately owned. The number of cannons each ship carried usually expressed the size of the king's ship, for example, a one hundred-gun ship. The merchant marine classified their ships by tons of burden.

The man-of-war was a three-masted, square-rigged vessel. The largest had three decks carrying between sixty and one hundred twenty guns with twenty-four pound cannon balls or higher. The smaller class man-of-war had two decks with forty or fifty guns with up to eighteen-pounders. The frigate was also a three-masted, square-rigged vessel. It carried between twenty-four and thirty-six guns with eight, nine, or twelve-pounders. Frigates were usually lighter and faster. The flute was a cargo vessel and carried eight to thirty guns and was flat bottomed. The corvette was a smaller frigate, and was armed and served as a messenger ship. Barges were used to load and unload goods, passengers, and cannons between the wharf and the larger ships anchored in the harbor.

Frigates' and flutes' draughts were shallower than men-of-war, usually around thirteen to fourteen feet. Men-of-war had seventeen to twenty-foot draughts. For this reason men-of-war had to stay one or two leagues off shore or in a deep harbor. Some of the larger frigates had to do the same.

Flutes transported men and supplies. Frigates carried mail and provided armed escort for convoys of ships crossing the Atlantic. Men-of-war were fighting ships and did escort duty during wartime. The royal navy fought the wars at sea for the kingdom in both the Old and New Worlds. The main enemy in the New World was England. The largest fighting ships were the ships of the line, and they used a fighting technique called a broadside. They would form a line of battle or column of ships, one behind the other. When the enemy ships were in range, they fired all of their guns on the side of the ship facing the enemy. The chance of a direct hit on the enemy was much greater. To destroy the enemy ship's mast, they often used a chain-shot—two metal balls attached by a foot long of chain. Men-of-war and frigates carried passengers and goods during peacetime. The captain would often remove most guns from one or two decks to accommodate passengers and cargo. However, these ships were not designed to transport passengers, only cargo and crew. In addition, the men-of-war were not designed to carry that much cargo, usually only enough to feed its crew and provide powder and ammunition for the guns.

Merchant marine frigates had a maximum capacity of five hundred to eight hundred tons of burden and the smaller tonnage ships, anywhere from twenty to one hundred fifty tons. Most were armed with a few guns. The smaller ships were used for coastal trade. Smaller ships were moored to piers, which extended into the harbor.

Chapter Eleven

All sailing ships had to go through a major refit each time they left for an Atlantic crossing, whether the ship was old or new. The process was called "careening." The rough seas, salt water, and woodworms took their toll during each sailing. The process of careening would start by removing the ballast in the hull of the ship, consisting of barrels of gravel, stones, and old iron. The rigging and sails were also removed. The ship was laid on its side to expose the hull by heaving it down using cables running through pulleys attached to the heads of the lower mast and then to capstans on the wharf. Workmen replaced rotten planks, sealed seams and cracks with oakum, and poured in pitch and hot tar to waterproof the hull. They also scraped and painted the surface portion of the hull and upper deck. The procedure was repeated for the other side of the ship. Once the ship was upright, they reloaded the ballast in the hull of the ship to help maintain its draft. An experienced captain determined the quantity and location of the ballast as it greatly influenced the speed and handling of the ship. Provisions and cargo were used as ballast, too. During the voyage, when casks of wine and water were consumed, they were refilled with seawater to maintain the ship's equilibrium. Sometimes the cannons were lowered into the hold for smoother sailing.

Careening and ballasting took three to four weeks. After the crew climbed the masts and reattached the rigging and sails, the ship was ready for cargo and passengers. The loading took about ten days. Men-of-war and merchant frigates could not enter shallow ports for loading of cargo. The workmen had to use barges in France to load and unload ships and bateauxs in New France. Cargo was taken in or out of the hold and between decks using block and tackle. Spaces between casks were filled with wooden blocks to prevent their movement during the trip. Provisions were placed in the staterooms and officers' quarters. Perishable items were stored in a room with plastered walls draped with fabric to keep out the water, and usually under lock and key. The quality of the casks and packing were sometimes poor. Poorly-packed goods had little protection against the dampness during the voyage. Intendants in New France required muskets and swords packed in cases wrapped in canvas to prevent rusting. Once in Canada or Louisiana, reloading took about the same number of days. Often, the colonists lacked sufficient goods to refill the ship for its sailing back to France.

Fitting out a ship was costly and required considerable manpower. Various merchants transported the cargo and provisions to the wharf. Laborers, boatmen, and barge skippers took the cargo to the vessel. Then there was the ship's crew. The largest men-of-war could have 600 to 700 crewmembers. The smaller men-of war and larger frigates could have 200 to 300 crewmembers. The smaller the ship, the smaller the number of its crew. Most merchant marine ships of comparable size had smaller crews than the king's ships. This was the result of the profit motive of the merchants. The cost of a six-month trip to New France and back was enormous. Costs for the various workers, supplies, provisions, munitions, and wages for the crew could exceed two hundred fifty thousand livres for a man-of-war, one hundred thirty thousand for a frigate, and ninety-five thousand for a flute.

After careening, the remaining work of fitting out the ship was performed by the crew. They remained onboard during loading and unloading. The crew was lodged and fed onboard. The captain took care of all the legal formalities such as permission to enter and leave ports and port duties. He was required to maintain a statement of his cargo and a passenger list. When the fitting out was complete, a representative of the Crown's Minister of Marine inspected the ship and allowed the boarding of passengers.

Traveling across the Atlantic was a risky and uncertain business. The voyage was dangerous. Navigational charts were not accurate and navigational instruments were rudimentary. The navigators used compasses and instruments to determine latitude and longitude. They made log entries at sunrise, mid-day, and sunset. Every half-hour during a crewmember's four-hour duty, a reading was taken with the renard (circular, wooden, or copper plate, which enables the helmsman to keep a record of wind conditions by inserting pegs at specific positions). They also used the positions of stars at night with instruments such as the astrolabe, the cross-staff, and the quadrant. Piracy and enemy war ships during times of war were a constant threat. The most important factor was, of course, the wind. A captain often had to wait for the right wind and tide to leave port. The time of year, ocean currents, and the strength of the winds determined the time for the crossing. It could take anywhere from forty-eight days to three months.

Pierre, Francois, Marie, and Landis found a large table in the corner of the tavern for supper. Two drunken sailors, who were being rowdy at the bar, left as they sat down. The establishment was not crowded yet. Most patrons dined or drank after the day's work was done. In this port city, that was not until the sun began to set.

"I hope Adrien didn't forget supper," said Pierre.

"That damned Minister Dubois better make good on his promise. I am getting very worried for you, Pierre," said his father. At that moment, Adrien walked into the tavern, and Pierre introduced him to his mother and Landis.

"Well, tomorrow the journey begins. Here are your shoes," said Adrien. "Are you ready, Pierre?"

"No, I don't want to go. I had a comfortable life in Maintenay," said Pierre as he tried on his new shoes. "Why are you so happy about going?"

"I am happier about getting away from here than going to the Louisiana colony, but I want to own my own farm one day," said Adrien. "I started out on a king's man-of war, *Le Dauphin Royal*, as a ship's boy when I was thirteen, just as the war was ending. My father died in the War of the Spanish Succession. My mother and I moved to La Rochelle to find work. Seaman's work was the only work I could find at that age, so I became a ship's boy to help support my mother and me. I was paid only three or four livres a month, but I got to save it all because I lived and ate on the ship. My mother was a domestic."

"Where is your mother now?" asked Marie.

"I don't really know. I returned from a voyage one day and she was gone. She drank something awful. Some said she ran off with a sailor. I have been on my own ever since, some four or five years now."

"How did you survive?" asked Francois.

"Mr. Legros, the shoemaker, gave me a place to stay in the back of his shop. I have been living there between voyages and learning the trades of a cobbler and tailor. What about you, Pierre? You look to be from too fine a family to be a convict."

Pierre told Adrien his life story: from having tutors and working on his father's tax farm to the night he and Simone robbed Antoine Patin and landed himself in prison. He had gone along with the robbery as a joke, but it was no joke now. He knew his life was about to take a major detour, whether he was ready for it or not. "I thought about running away with Simone to Italy, but father, I just could not put you in that position," said Pierre looking down at the table, dejected.

As he was about to explain prison life, a man wearing a hat, long-sleeved shirt, pants, and boots, and covered with dust, entered the tavern.

"Anyone here by the name of Francois Mayeux?" asked the stranger. Francois was somewhat taken aback. Why would someone be asking for him?

"Yes, that would be me," said Francois as he rose from his seat and approached the man.

"The innkeeper told me you might be here. I have a letter to you from Minister Dubois. I think you have something for him in your possession?" said the stranger as he handed the letter to Francois. Francois ripped open the wax seal with the insignia of John Law and began to read to himself. His fatigue turned to contentment.

"Everyone stay here. I will be right back. Follow me," Francois told the stranger as he handed the letter to Pierre. Francois left the tavern and went into the lobby of the Pontchartrain Inn. He asked the innkeeper to retrieve the two sets of books from the iron chest behind the counter. Francois had placed them there upon his arrival in La Rochelle for safe keeping. He handed them to the stranger.

After a cursory review of the books, the stranger walked out of the inn, climbed on his horse, and rode off without saying a word. Francois knew at that moment, he had done all he could for his son. Pierre was now a man living on his own.

"Did Pierre tell you the good news?" Francois hollered to his supper guests as he returned to the tavern. Everyone had begun to eat. Fish was for supper. "Pierre will be going to the Louisiana colony as an engage for John Law's personal concession at the Arkansas post. He will be working as an accountant at the post warehouse with the storekeeper. Landis, get us a small cask of brandy."

The drinks flowed freely. Marie had enough of the excitement for the day and went back to the inn early to get some sleep. Tomorrow would be a depressing day for her. Her baby boy would be leaving, and it was a possibility that she would never to see him again. The whole episode felt more like a funeral than a going away party. The brandy withdrew everyone's worries and inhibitions and the words came without restraint. Landis was drunk and almost started a fight with a sailor at the bar, but the other three persuaded everyone to get back to drinking.

"Don't give him any more brandy," said Francois as he pointed to Landis. He had become quiet and was swaying on his chair with a permanent fixation on a painting of a ship hanging on the wall as if he were a crewmember in action on its deck.

"How did you get on the *Le Dauphin Royal* as a ship's boy?" asked Pierre.

"My mother signed me up," said Adrien.

"Signed up for what?" asked Pierre.

"The Navel Code," said Adrien.

"He's talking about the *Code des Armees Navales*. Louis XIV's Minister of the Navy promulgated the code in 1689 to govern all operations of the French fleet of royal ships and merchant ships," said Francois.

"That's it," said Adrien. "All males between the ages of fifteen and fifty who are living in coastal towns are required to register with the Ministry of the Navy. We were assigned to one of four classes. Every four years, each class had to serve one year on the king's vessels. The other three years, we could serve on merchant ships for more pay. But, the captain of a royal ship can commandeer sailors from merchant ships to fill out their crews if they are short or in war time. I worked my way up from an ordinary seaman to an able seaman," explained Adrien.

"That code was decreed mostly for periods of war," said Francois.

"Why aren't we registered?" asked Pierre. "We live only ten leagues from the town of Berck, on the coast."

"Because we are tax farmers, not sailors. I got an exemption for me, you, and your brother," said Francois.

"I wish I could have sailed. Now I know nothing about this voyage," said Pierre.

"I know us sailors don't make much, about twenty-five livres a month on a king's ship as an able seaman. That's about what a soldier makes in the Louisiana colony. Ordinary seamen make less than that," said Adrien. "I think I will head back to the shop. See you at the wharf early. Thanks for supper, Monsieur Mayeux."

Francois and Pierre stayed at the tavern for a while longer. Francois encouraged Pierre to stay close to Adrien on the voyage and follow his advice and lead. He could tell that Adrien was a good and honest young man. He advised him to keep his silver under lock and key in his chest while on the ship. He asked Pierre to write home often, especially for the sake of his mother. He thanked him for facing these trials like a man and not running off to Italy. After they embraced, they managed to get Landis to stir enough to get him across the street and to bed.

The next morning Francois was up early, as usual. He managed to shave with his straight knife and the bowl and water provided by the inn. The accommodations were surely not that of home. Marie was up and dressed and went over to the room occupied by Pierre and Landis to get them up. Both were still sleeping. Pierre answered the door. Landis had the hang arounds from the night before and was in no mood to greet the morning.

"We are off to breakfast. Do you have all your things packed?" asked Marie.

"Yes, I only have a few changes of clothes, a couple of pairs of shoes, a few books and writing paper, quill and ink," said Pierre.

"Do you have the livre your father gave you?"

"Not yet. I guess he will give it to me when he settles the charges with the innkeeper. I think he has it stored in the innkeeper's iron chest," said Pierre.

"I will miss you so much," said Marie as she sobbed and gave Pierre a hug. "I don't know what I will do with myself with you not at the house. Our home will surely feel empty."

"Mother, we will both make it through this. I hope to be back in three years after I finish my engagement with the John Law concession. Let's meet Father for breakfast," said Pierre as he glanced at Landis still sleeping in the bed. "I think we will leave him here."

Francois was already at the tavern eating when Marie and Pierre entered. "You better eat a large breakfast. This may be the last good meal you get for a while," said Francois before realizing that this was not the most encouraging thing to say to his son under the circumstances. Francois paid for everyone's breakfast. He left Marie and Pierre eating and went back to the inn to retrieve Pierre's silver. He had managed to stuff five-thousand-livre worth of silver coins in two cloth bags with just enough excess cloth at the top of the bag to tie it closed with string. When he returned to the tavern, Pierre and Marie were done eating. "Here, put this in your chest and keep it under lock and key. That is a year-and-a-half worth of wages for a sailor," said Francois.

"I will not be a sailor for a year and a half," said Pierre in rebuttal. "Let's get to the wharf. Adrien is to meet us there early."

Dawn had made an early exit, and the sun was fully up. The coolness of the night was wearing off and the warmth of the day was setting in. The sea gulls sang their morning serenades. The salty air whirled about with the aid of a constant, coastal sea breeze. The wharf was full of activity already, just as the day before, with the tradesmen and artisans busy at work. Except this time something was a little different.

Women in bonnets with long flowing dresses of various colors were milling about the wharf with their male companions. The passengers of the *La Profond* were gathering around the posted passenger list as Pierre and his family approached. Pierre's interest was immediately drawn to one female passenger in a yellow dress. Her yellow bonnet held down her long, flowing auburn hair as it tossed in the morning breeze. Her speech and youthful gaiety kept the older women around her mesmerized. Pierre made his way through the crowd to get a closer look and purposely brushed against her. She gave him a cool glance and a smile. Pierre returned the smile and knew, at that moment, he was in love. Somehow, the fact that the passenger list was rewritten with his name listed as an engage for John Law's concession did not matter to him as much anymore. Simone seemed to be a distant memory. Pierre's mother brought him back to reality when she came up to him and stuffed a biscuit in his coat pocket.

"You may need this on the ship," said Marie as Pierre alternatively stared at the beautiful, young passenger and searched the crowd for

Adrien. "Calm down. Adrien will be here. I will be sitting on that bale of cotton if your father is looking for me."

"There is Adrien," said Pierre to his mother as he rushed over to greet him good morning. "Where have you been?"

"I had last minute business to take care of," said Adrien. "It will take a while for the crew to load all the passengers and their luggage," said Adrien as Francois walked up.

"I see that the captain moored the ship next to the pier extending into the harbor. The tide is up. The gangplank has been lowered into place," said Francois. "Passengers are starting to board. Luckily for the ladies, they won't have to be ferried to the ship."

"Let's board," said Pierre. The trip had now taken on an excitement of its own for Pierre. The embarrassment of his conviction had slipped away and he began a personal reflection on his future. He was stepping into manhood. He gave his mother and father a final kiss and embrace. All the words that could have been spoken had already been said. It was time to go. Marie began to cry. Landis finally approached, still in a drunken stupor, and gave Pierre a handshake.

Pierre grabbed his traveling chest and threw it on his shoulder. Adrien had a small leather satchel containing all of his worldly possessions. As they began to approach the gangplank, Pierre noticed the girl in the yellow dress having difficulty with her bags. Pierre glanced over at Adrien with a smile, then made his way to her.

"May I help you with your bags?" asked Pierre.

"Yes, please," said the girl. "It seems that Mother had me pack more than I needed."

"My name is Pierre Mayeux. It is my pleasure to be of service."

"My name is Marie Sellier. I'm traveling with my mother and father to the Louisiana colony. Father was recently appointed deputy intendant for the Mississippi Company."

"Marie is a lovely name. That is the name of my mother. I will be working for John Law's concession at the Arkansas post," said Pierre as he grabbed her two bags and threw his chest on his shoulder. He could have carried a hogshead full of salted meat with the energy running through his body. "Meet my friend, Adrien LeBeau," said Pierre as Adrien approached. "Adrien, this is Marie Sellier."

'Pleased to meet you, Ms. Sellier," said Adrien. "Have you ever sailed before?"

"No, this is my first time on a ship. I am so scared," said Marie.

"Everything will be fine," said Pierre as they made their way up the gangplank. Marie's mother and father were already onboard. A crewmember was directing passengers to their quarters as they reached the top deck. Most of the passengers had dropped their baggage and were along the rail waving at family and friends on the wharf.

Pierre located his mother, father, and Landis and he and Adrien began to wave, too. Sadness overcame him. He wondered if he would ever see his mother and father again, or France for that matter. At that moment, Marie grabbed his hand as if she could feel his pain and she began waving, too, with her other hand. Joy and happiness returned to Pierre.

"The captain has hoisted the flag on the topmast. We are about ready to raise anchor," said Adrien.

Marie was startled when she heard a cannon go off. "What was that?" she asked.

"That was a five-pounder announcing our departure. The captain will soon give the order to unfurl the topsail for casting off. If anyone else is planning on going to the New World on the *La Profond*, they better get aboard," said Adrien.

"Looks like we have good winds this morning," said Pierre as the flag on the topmast cracked in the wind. It was now full watch. All crew were at their posts. The anchor master barked orders to his crew. As they heaved the chain and anchor onto the deck, the rumbling of the chain shuddered throughout the ship. Seamen were in the rigging unfurling the sails. The master pilot had the ship's course plotted out. Once the sails were hoisted, trimmed and lowered, some eighteen to twenty of them, they filled with wind and the ship was cast off.

✤

The Company granted a large number of concessions in 1718, 1719, and 1720. The D'Ancenis concession was located sixteen leagues above New Orleans. The organizers were Marquis d'Ancenis, Lieutenant General of the Pacardie Province in France. They shipped one hundred thirteen persons under the control of a director from France on the ship *La Seine* in 1720. The D'Artagnan concession was formed by Count d'Artagnan, captain of the king's Musketeers and commandant general of the city of Nimes, France. His concession was located six leagues above the city of New Orleans on the left bank of the Mississippi River and became known as Cannes Brulees (Burnt Cane). Daniel Kolly, a member of the Financial Council of Bavaria and others, organized the Kolly concession. They shipped three hundred six persons from France on the *Le St. Andre* in May of 1720. His concession was also known as St. Catherine. It was located near the Natchez post and Fort Rosalie among the Natchez Indians. Jean Baptiste Benard de la Harpe started a concession two hundred thirty-six leagues above New Orleans when he personally brought over forty workers onboard the *La Victoire* in August 1718. La Harpe owned another concession eleven leagues above New Orleans on the right bank of the Mississippi. John Law established his concession at the mouth of the Arkansas River as it emptied into the Mississippi River. He spared no expense, as he had become one of the wealthiest nobles of Paris. Over a period of time, he sent over fifteen hundred Germans from the Rhineland to establish the concession. He committed over one and a half million livres of goods to his concession and intended to establish a city there according to Father Du Poisson, a Jesuit missionary assigned to the post. However, John Law's hasty departure from the scene would eventually strain those lofty hopes and dreams.

Chapter Twelve

The passengers were jolted as the ship lurched forward from its slumber. The three masts of sails full of wind on this tall ship was a beautiful sight to the well-wishers on the wharf. The captain and his lieutenant and midshipmen were yelling orders as the ship passed the towers guarding the harbor and turned south along the French coast into the open Atlantic.

Some time later, Adrien was explaining the details of sailing a ship.

"Captains try to keep a course between the forty-third and forty-seventh parallels when sailing to Canada so they can hit the Grand Banks," he said. "I don't think we will be taking the northern route though. We will probably sail south to the west coast of Africa and catch the northeast trade winds. The easterlies and sea currents bring you right into the Caribbean in the summer months. All ships returning to France, even the ones from the Louisiana colony, sail to the Grand Banks off Newfoundland to take advantage of the prevailing westerly winds and currents year round.

"Westerly winds do not move toward the west, they move from the west to the east just as the easterlies move from the east to the west. A crossing from Newfoundland back to France can take only thirty days with the right winds. The westerlies blow hardest in the fall and winter but don't be caught up there between November and March. The ice is very dangerous."

"It seems there are only six good months for making the crossing. Now I can see why news from the New World travels so slowly. How many leagues do we travel a day?" asked Pierre.

"The navigator ties a piece of wood to the end of a rope with knots tied for forty-seven feet at six inches apart. The navigator will throw out the wood and count the number of knots released during thirty seconds of the hourglass. The number of knots let out equals the number of leagues traveled per hour. But it all depends on the wind, an average of twenty to thirty leagues a day. The most I have ever seen is fifty leagues. Sometimes we have contrary winds and have to tack. On one trip to the New World, we were traveling west into the setting sun. The next morning, we woke up heading into the rising sun," said Adrien. They all got a good laugh out of that.

"I pray to God we do *not* have bad weather," said Marie. "I'm still trying to find my sea legs. Many of the women and some of the men are sea sick already."

"Stormy weather can make things difficult. You can't sleep or eat. You get tossed around to the point of wanting to tie yourself to something. When it rains, water leaks through the top deck and everything gets wet. The hold of the ship fills with water and the crew has to start pumping. There is the pump next to the main mast. The piston down below pushes the water up here and the water is swept over the top deck. Two sailors man the pump, one on each end. Pumping is a tiresome job," said Adrien.

"It sounds as though you have been on a ship before. How long will it take us to get to the Louisiana colony?" asked Marie.

"About sixty days," said Adrien.

"That's a long time in such a confined space," said Marie. "I may go stark, raving mad."

"I have been sailing six or seven years now, never had any formal tutoring. I can write and read a little. Between voyages, I have been learning the trades of shoemaker and tailor," said Adrien.

"Marie and I will tutor you if you get us through this voyage," said Pierre.

"Pierre, you must meet my parents. Let's find them," said Marie.

Marie lead Pierre to the other side of the top deck where her parents were gazing out into the open Atlantic, surely questioning their decision to leave France for the New World. The salty, ocean air rushed across the top deck as it pushed the ship along. The crew was still busy adjusting the sails to efficiently capture the wind. The captain and his navigator were at the wheel on the quarterdeck. The noise of the rudder changed ever so slowly to adjust course.

"Mother and Father, I want you to meet my new friend, Pierre Mayeux. Pierre this is Monsieur Jean Sellier and Madame Annabel Sellier," said Marie.

"Pleased to meet you, Pierre. What brings you on this voyage?" asked Monsieur Sellier.

"I am an employee of the Mississippi Company at the John Law concession at the Arkansas post," said Pierre.

"Yes, Father, he is the son of a tax farmer in Picardy."

"We have relatives in the Picardy Province," said Madame Sellier. "You must have received a good education being from a family of a tax farmer?"

"Yes, I was fortunate to have two wonderful tutors. I know a couple of languages, Spanish and English, and Latin of course. I was taught finance and was working with my father in his tax farm when I decided to come to the New World," said Pierre hoping his last few words would not haunt him in the Louisiana colony.

"You know, I have been appointed deputy intendant for the Louisiana colony by the directors of the Company. I could use your experience there. Come see me when we get settled in at Biloxi," said Monsieur Sellier.

"We are going to find our lodging," said Madame Sellier as the ship rolled to one side and Marie's mother lost her balance. Pierre had to catch her, otherwise, she would have fallen. "Thank you, Pierre. Come along, Marie. We have a cabin in the quarterdeck below the captain's quarters. There is also a galley and dining room for the captain, chief officers, and their guests."

"See you later, Marie," said Pierre as he looked around and found Adrien talking to some of the crew. Pierre strutted over to Adrien but wasn't listening to a word he said. His mind was on a little red-headed lady. "Where do we sleep?"

"Most of the cannons have been removed from the between-decks. We will be sleeping in hammocks strung from the ship's beams. It's nothing but a three by six-foot piece of canvas tied at each end. A midshipman once called them swinging graves because so many sailors died of scurvy on that voyage," said Adrien.

Pierre and Adrien went down below from the top deck to the between decks, of which there were two. They discovered that most of the passengers were on the first between deck. The crew was assigned to sleep on the second between deck. The ship's hold was below the sailors. A makeshift partition of canvas was strung up across one end of the first between deck—a relatively large open space—to give some privacy for the women onboard. The cannon portholes were open and provided the only light. One large cannon remained in place. Pierre and Adrien found a corner in the front of the ship, across from the lone cannon, and tied their hammocks.

"Not much head room, maybe five feet," hollered Pierre over the chatter of the passengers. "The cannon port hole lets in a nice breeze, though."

"This is huge compared to some of the merchant ships. Some have only three and a half feet of distance between the floor and ceiling," said Adrien. "Watch your head at night. Lanterns and candles are not permitted for fear of catching the ship on fire."

Pierre climbed into his hammock as it swayed from side to side with the rolling motion of the ship. The bed was not the soft feather mattress that he was used to at home, but it would suffice. Pierre could not get Marie out of his mind. Somehow, her beauty and effervescence masked the heartbreak of leaving his parents and Simone behind. The discomforts of the ship were only of minor concern now. He wondered what Marie was doing at that very minute.

⚜

"These are such cramped quarters, and it is so hot in here," said Madame Sellier. "Marie, you will have to sleep on the cot and your father and I will sleep in the bunk beds."

"Stop complaining, Mother. The paneling in the room keeps out most of the noises. Just think if we had to sleep with the other passengers in hammocks."

"Well, we are not other passengers, my dear," said Madame Sellier. "This sea sickness is getting the best of me."

"Ladies, calm down. This will be a long passage so let's start out with a good attitude. We all decided that I should take this position. We will have to live with the consequences," said Monsieur Sellier. "If this is the worst we encounter, count yourselves lucky."

"You better stay clear of that Mayeux boy," said Madame Sellier as she threw up again in a chamber pot.

"Oh, Mother. He seems to be such a nice gentleman. Something in him brought out something in me that I have never felt before. His manners are refined, and he is extremely educated."

"He is not nobility. I wonder about him," said Madame Sellier.

"We are no longer nobility either, mother," said Marie in an attempt to defend Pierre's honor. A knock came upon the door and the captain entered.

"Captain Pemanech, come in," said Monsieur Sellier.

"I hope your accommodations are suitable?" asked the captain.

"Oh yes, very nice," said Madame Sellier as she turned and looked at Marie.

"Which route shall we take to the colony?" asked Monsieur Sellier.

"We are heading south to the west coast of Africa. We will pass the Canary Islands. At Cape Verde Islands, off the coast of Senegal, we will head due west. The northeast trade winds should bring us to the leeward islands of the Caribbean. The pilot will hold a course on the fifteenth parallel, the Tropic of Cancer. Let's pray we have good winds with no storms," said Captain Pemanech.

"Have you made this passage before?" asked Marie.

"Oh yes, I have made the voyage several times now on different ships without any problems. No need to worry, young lady," said the captain. "I have assigned you to my table for meals. Dinner will be served at high noon. I hope to see you shortly, Monsieur Sellier."

Bells and drums announced dinner. Everyone on the ship ate at the same time. After the pilot took the noon reading of the sun (whenever it was not covered by clouds) the chaplain said grace on the top deck. The passengers ate along side the sailors and petty officers. The chief officers, chaplain, and the important passengers ate at the captain's table. His table was often set with ceramic bowls and servers, silver flatware and plates and tableware. Each diner was assigned a place at the table for the entire voyage so the servant could become accustomed to the diner's eating habits. The chaplain—required aboard all of the king's ships—said the Catholic Grace, always thanking God for the cook, a safe passage, and the king's health. The captain's dining room was under the quarterdeck in the rear of the ship. It also served as a meeting room for the chief officers. The kitchens for the captain's table and the crew were in the forecastle. The forecastle for the *La Profond* was a multi-decked structure in the front of the ship. Cooking was usually done in an open hearth made of cast iron and fastened to the deck. The fuel was wood. A smoke sail screened the chimney. The captain's table often had fresh meat taken from the animals brought onboard, usually chickens, pigs, sheep, and a few head of cattle. The cook prepared the seamens' meals in a large cauldron. On bad weather days, no one got hot cooked meals for fear of setting the ship on fire.

Marie excused herself from the dinner table before dessert. The excessive boastings and exaggerations of the captain's guests bored her. She ventured out to the top deck to find Pierre. Walking across the deck, she noticed a number of the crew and passengers were sitting and eating. Another shift of the crew were at work manning the sails. The sun was shining brightly and the deck was hot, but the strong sea breeze made for a pleasant afternoon. Marie found Pierre and Adrien sitting on a huge coil of rope and eating.

"How was dinner?" Pierre asked as Marie walked up.

"It was very good. We had a tureen of mutton soup and a chicken fricassee. We had fresh baked bread, butter, and cheese. I left before dessert. Dessert was some sort of stewed fruit and preserves. The captain just opened a cask of brandy as I excused myself," said Marie.

"The privileged class," said Pierre jokingly. "We are eating a seaman's diet. I understand that today is a flesh day—boiled meat with rice and vegetable broth."

"As opposed to fish day, I suppose," said Marie sarcastically.

"The meat was not soaked enough before cooking to extract the salt so it was much too salty," said Pierre. "This food will take some getting used to."

"We never get fresh meat onboard. It's always salted meat or cod fish from barrels," said Adrien. "Supper is no better. It will consist of cooked beans and usually the leftover broth from dinner."

"The drink is not too terribly bad–a quarter pint of wine with the remainder filled with water," said Pierre. "Fresh water is scarce on the ship–only enough for consumption. Beware, bathing is infrequent to non-existent."

"Breakfast is the worst," said Adrien. "Always two sea biscuits with wine and water. The petty officers do a little better. They may get a sardine, a little salted meat or cheese with their two sea biscuits. On bad weather days, its hard tack all day."

"What is hard tack?" asked Marie.

"Another name for sea biscuits," said Adrien. "They are made with pure wheat flour. They are shaped like pancakes and the dough is cooked into a flat biscuit of about eight ounces each. They are prepared weeks before the voyage and stored in sixty-pound sacks."

"That sounds awful. Look what I brought you, Pierre," said Marie. She revealed a piece of roasted meat from her pocket and handed it to Pierre. "It came from the captain's table."

"Roasted mutton, this is delicious," said Pierre as he handed a piece to Adrien. "What a sweet surprise you have been," said Pierre to Marie in the English language.

"What did you say?" asked Adrien who barely had command of his own French language.

"I was only thanking Marie for the treat in English," said Pierre.

"English, I hate the English," said Adrien.

"I hope these precious days I spend with you on this ship never end. Meet me tonight on the top deck after supper," said Pierre to Marie in English again. Adrien only looked confused.

Marie nodded her head in agreement. Marie and Pierre looked forward to spending the afternoon together. Instead, they had to entertain Adrien as he told them stories about his sailing adventures. The afternoon turned into early evening. The crew stayed busy all afternoon hoisting and trimming sails. Marie finally decided that she needed to meet her parents for supper.

Pierre and Adrien ate supper with the rest of the passengers and crew. The crew changed shifts at six p.m. at the sound of drums and bells. Supper was a light meal. The heavy meal of the day aboard ship was dinner, at noon. The dishes had not been washed well because of the lack of water on board. They were wrapped in greasy rags to keep them from being thrown about the ship. These greasy rags also kept the eating utensils from rusting due to exposure to salt water. After supper, Pierre and Adrien walked about the ship. Adrien began to give Pierre a lesson in seamanship.

"The crew is divided into two groups. One group is responsible for the portside and the other group is responsible for the starboard side. A crew from each group rotates shifts every four hours. A sailor's work schedule is four hours on and four hours off, twenty-four hours a day," said Adrien.

"Sounds as though when they are off duty, they usually eat or sleep," said Pierre.

"Yes, a seaman does not have much to do off duty. They are prohibited from gambling during the voyage. One third of their wages are paid at the end of the voyage so if they have infractions, they don't get their final payment," said Adrien.

"Are the captain and chief officers paid well?" asked Pierre.

"About one hundred to one hundred fifty livres per month for chief officers and three hundred livres per month for the captain. In violation of the naval code, they often carry extra merchandise on the ship to sell in the colonies. Hams, cheeses and casks of wine and brandy can command a good price in the colonies," said Adrien.

"Does the navel code stipulate the number of officers and petty officers on a ship?" asked Pierre.

"Yes, besides the captain there are the lieutenants, midshipman, a surgeon, a writer, chaplain and pilot. Petty officers include the master carpenter, the master gunner, the master caulker, and the master cook. During wartime, the code requires two men to operate a four-pound cannon, seven men for a twelve pounder, nine men for eighteen and twenty-four pounders, and fifteen men for thirty-six pounders. The master gunner inspects the cannons, arranges cannon balls by caliber, prepares charges for firing the guns, and keeps the powder dry. The master carpenter repairs planks and leaks in the ship and also handles cobbler duties," said Adrien.

They walked the ship from bow to stern inspecting all the nooks and crannies as they ate their meager supper. The lesson finally ended when it became dark. They watched the sun disappear over the western horizon. It extinguished itself as it dropped into the ocean. The setting sun confirmed to them that they were still heading south.

"I think I will go below, to my hammock," said Adrien.

"I think I will stay up a little longer. See you in the morning, my friend," said Pierre.

"Missing home already?" asked Adrien.

"Something like that," said Pierre.

The ship had finally become quiet. The sails could be heard flapping in the wind. Most of the passengers had gone to bed. Only a few sailors could be heard laughing and petty officers barking orders. The heat of the day had finally dissipated, and the coolness of the night had set in over the open ocean. Every few minutes a wave could be heard crashing against the bow as the ship made headway. Pierre was alone. He did not think about home. He waited with excited anticipation for Marie's arrival. He was beginning to think that she would not come.

Then he heard, "Pierre, Pierre," coming from a silhouette whispering in the starlit night. "I had to wait until Mother and Father went to sleep to slip out," said Marie.

"I was beginning to think that you forgot," said Pierre who took her hand as they walked along the side rail on the top deck of the ship. The moon had already set. Marie's face was aglow with the light from the heaven of a thousand twinkling stars. They each had a hold of the other's heart and were at a place that could never be dark—a state of grace.

"A strange feeling came over me when I first saw you on the wharf in La Rochelle," said Pierre.

"I felt the same way," said Marie. "It's as if a part of me is only for you. I have never felt that way before. Have you?" asked Marie.

"I thought I was in love with a girl in Maintenay. Her name is Simone. I know now it was not love, only lust," said Pierre.

"Would you be true to me?" asked Marie.

"I am free to love you, only you, Marie," said Pierre. His heart beat wildly.

Marie responded to Pierre's embrace. Their mouths met for a passionate kiss, then another and another. Pierre nibbled on her neck and ear. He could feel the tingle running through her body.

"We must stop," said Marie. "We cannot do anything on this ship. Anyway, I am saving myself for my husband."

"You are right. This ship is no place for lovers. Let's wait for the perfect time and place," said Pierre as he put his arm around her and she put her arm around him. They looked to the heavens as if to confirm that God himself had placed them there together on the *La Profond*, bound to the New World.

"Did you see that shooting star?" asked Marie as they walked toward the quarterdeck.

"No," said Pierre. "The stars are so bright tonight. Look at the pilot. He is reading the stars."

"Will he find our future together in the heavens?" asked Marie.

"You are my shooting star, Marie. I will follow you anywhere. You are my North Star by night and my sun by day," said Pierre.

Pierre escorted Marie to her cabin, even knowing that he would face the captain's wrath as well as Monsieur and Madam Sellier's if they caught him there. After another kiss goodnight, he was off to find his hammock. The between deck was pitch black, hot, and steamy. The crew closed almost all of the cannon ports in case of rain. Excessive rain could sink a ship. Pierre could only make his way by touch. He had to bend over so as not to hit his head on the beams of the low ceiling. He finally found his hammock and crawled in. He could not sleep even though the ship was rocking him like a baby in a cradle. He could only think of Marie. Her voice in his head easily distracted him from the snoring of the room full of passengers and the awful smells coming from the hold of the ship.

The hours on ship turned into days, and the days turned into weeks. The misery suffered by most of the passengers was just another day's work for the crew. Pierre suffered neither the rigors of the passengers nor the toils of the crew. He was the happiest he had ever been. He was in love. Nights were spent longing for Marie and days were spent courting and romancing her within the captive walls aboard ship. The voyage began a glorious new chapter in his life, but he wondered, with exceedingly high expectations if Marie was going to be its fulfillment.

When John Law's Mississippi Company took over the administration of the Louisiana colony in 1717 after Crozat returned it to the Crown, the seat of government in the colony at the time was at Mobile. Bienville was appointed commandant general for the third time in 1718 after Lepinay was sacked. Bienville would remain in that position until 1725. Bienville transferred the capital from Mobile to the gulf coast at New Biloxi in 1719. In October of 1718, Bienville got permission from the directors of the Mississippi Company to build a deep-water port on the Mississippi River. The board of directors approved of the location of Nouvelle Orleans thirty leagues above the mouth of the Mississippi River. The royal engineer was dispatched to the colony with instructions to build the city at Bayou Iberville (Manchac), where it emptied into the Mississippi River. The Manchac site was on high ground and not subject to inundation from the river. It also provided a direct water route from the Mississippi River to Lake Maurapas. Bienville desired a different site, a crescent in the Mississippi, which could be easily defended from ships coming up or going down the river. The site was north of the forts at the English Turn but south of Bayou Iberville (Manchac). Most importantly, the site was within portage distance to Bayou St. Jean and Lake Pontchartrain, thus considered an ideal trading post by Bienville.

The French built a small fort, St. Jean, on the bank of Lake Pontchartrain at the mouth of Bayou St. Jean in 1701. The natives and French fur traders (courtiers de bois) used Bayou St. Jean (called Bayou Choupigue by the natives) as a trade route between the Mississippi River and Lake Pontchartrain. The headwater, or beginning of the bayou, was only a short distance from the site of Bienville's port on the Mississippi River. The Indians created a portage to carry their boats the short distance from Bayou St. Jean to the Mississippi River. Bienville figured if it was good for the Indians, it would be good for the French.

Construction of Nouvelle Orleans on the bank of the Mississippi River started in March of 1718 when a few huts covered with palmetto prawns and storage houses were built so troops and supplies could be moved from Mobile. The royal engineer, La Tour, who was sent from France to aid in the location and design of the city, had disputed Bienville's choice, but Bienville had already begun construction. Bienville chose Adrian de Pauger, a royal engineer in the colony, to design the city. The city was laid out in a grid pattern, six blocks deep and eleven blocks long with the rectangle perpendicular to the river. The streets were named after the royal houses of France and Catholic saints with such names as Bourbon, Dauphine, Royal, Iberville, Bienville, Orleans, Dumaine, Conti, Toulouse,

Burgundy, and St. Louis, St. Ann, St. Peter and St. Phillip. The city was named New Orleans (Nouvelle Orleans) after the Regent of France, Philippe II, Duke of Orleans.

The city had a slow beginning. The quay, the land between the river and the city, was reserved for wharves and business purposes. The streets were laid out into sixty-six blocks, each block fifty square toises with twelve emplacements for lodging. By 1720, only eight blocks by three blocks (a total of twenty-four blocks) had been cleared and laid out, facing the river. Woods still surrounded the city. The Place d'Armes was the center block used as the parade ground for the troops. The side of the square parade ground facing the river was to remain open to the river. The block immediately behind the Place d'Armes was reserved for the parish church, St. Louis Cathedral. A house of the Capuchins, who would officiate Mass, was to the left of the church. To the right of the church was the prison and guardhouse. The Mississippi Company warehouse and the house of the deputy intendant sat in the block to the left of the parade ground, and the government house sat in the block to the right. On each side of the parade ground were rows of barracks. Commandant General Bienville's house sat in the middle of town. The Urseline nuns and the hospital were in the block to the far right of the city, facing the river. Houses built of brick and timber began to slowly appear. A road was built to the north of the city to connect to Bayou St. Jean.

Because of continued inundation, especially during the early spring, ditches were dug along each street running away from the river as the land had a gentle slope toward Lake Pontchartrain. Bienville finally forced concession owners on each side of the river to construct a small levee about three to four feet high and wide enough to drive a carriage on the top. They objected to such work for the Company but were threatened with the loss of their slaves, so the concession owners put the slaves to work constructing levees. The levee system ran from the English Turn to ten leagues north of the city. The road at the base of the levee was a very smooth travel by coach. Habitations began to spring up all along the river on both sides. Bienville personally managed his large concession across the river from New Orleans. A census of the Louisiana colony in 1721 showed a population of about twenty-five hundred persons of Europeans descent, including engages. Negro slaves and Indian slaves numbered about fifteen hundred. These figures did not include the five hundred or so soldiers and military personnel, depending on deaths and desertions.

Chapter Thirteen

The boy king, Louis XV, as all princes, was placed in the care of a man when he reached his seventh birthday. Louis XV was taken from his governess, Madame de Ventadour, in February 1717, and placed in the care of his governor, Francois de Villeroy, in the nearby Tuileries Palace. Cardinal de Fleury served as the king's tutor. Because he was only seven years old, the Regent, Philippe II, was still acting on behalf of the king. The Regent was the current power broker and the divinity of the young King had somehow migrated to Philippe II. The boy king was virtually unaware of the financial condition of France in August of 1720.

John Law's financial genius emerged way before its time. He had envisioned a financial system whereby only paper money would be used as a means of exchange, not gold and silver. Banks would make loans with paper money and the whole economy would efficiently operate under such a system. But the weak spot in Law's scheme had been exposed: his willingness to issue more and more banknotes to fund purchases of shares in the Mississippi Company. The Crown steadily printed banknotes that were not backed by sufficient amounts of gold and silver coins (specie). The banknotes flooded the economy. The public clamored for these banknotes to purchase shares in the Mississippi Company. Share prices had risen to eighteen thousand livres per share. Inflation for goods and services was steadily rising. John Law had created the Mississippi Bubble.

But financial savvy and greed quickly tempered the mayhem. Foreign investors and witty Frenchmen began quietly selling shares at or near the peak and withdrew specie from the bank. Stock prices began falling from January through April 1720 as some of the investing public sold shares to turn capital gains into gold coin. In an attempt to stop the sell-off, Law restricted any payment in gold and silver that was more than one hundred livres.

Gold and silver was leaving the royal bank and was being hoarded or taken out of the kingdom. An edict was issued to outlaw anyone who had in his possession over five hundred livres in gold or silver. Not even goldsmiths or the clergy were exempt. A new term emerged: realizers. These were the people who had realized the coming misfortune and cashed in their shares for specie before the troubles began. The realizers turned to real estate, furniture, or anything with solid value. Members of the Parlement de Paris had become hostile to the Crown. Chancellor d'Aguesseau wanted John Law hanged.

In May 1720, Law devalued shares in the company in several monthly stages. Share prices went from nine thousand livres to five thousand. He also devalued the banknotes. The value of banknotes was reduced to 50 percent of their face value. To alleviate the financial burden on smaller investors, the banknotes remained legal tender at their original face value for payment of taxes. At these prices the bank would exchange shares for banknotes or banknotes for shares. Two bureaus were opened. The investing public swarmed them with their shares and demanded banknotes in exchange. The bank became the owner of a large number of its own shares. But the promise that the banknotes would remain stable was broken by the Crown.

Law was fired on May 28 and placed under house arrest. The regent ordered a regiment of the royal guard to protect Law from the fury of the crowds. But within days Law was freed and resumed his seat in the cabinet. The regent had no idea what to do and realized that if France was to be saved, only John Law could execute the redemption. The regent owned one hundred thousand shares subscribed at five thousand livres. He had a paper profit in January 1720 of five hundred million livres. It is doubtful if he realized any of this. By December 1720, his shares were basically worthless.

When Law returned, his primary goal was to reduce the number of banknotes in circulation and save the Company from bankruptcy. In July of 1720 a royal edict was issued. Law decided to issue bonds in the Mississippi Company backed by the Crown in exchange for banknotes. Some holders of banknotes participated but the program was ultimately unsuccessful. The public realized that the bonds issued by the Crown were just as worthless.

In an effort to slow the run on the Royal Bank, Law decided to allow banks to redeem notes for coins, but only in small denominations. Specie was so scarce, bank officers would insert clerks in the line who would return the money they withdrew. At one point the bank refused to accept anything but ten-livre notes. None of these remedies were able to build confidence in the banknotes or slow the panic-stricken investors in the Mississippi Company. In a last-ditch effort to restore confidence in the banking system, Law ordered the public burning of banknotes as they came in for redemption. This scheme sought to convince the public that the growing scarcity of notes would cause them to be worth more. Huge pits were set up outside the banks and several times a day, with great ceremony, the banknotes were sent to the funeral pyre. This went on during the months of July and August 1720 while the banknotes and share prices continued to lose value.

The whole system began to collapse under uncertainty. The value of banknotes and share prices plummeted. Everyone went to the bank to beg for specie. Soldiers were deployed to keep peace. The rush to convert paper money to coins led to sporadic bank hours and riots. Squatters occupied the square of Palace Louis-le-Grand and openly attacked the financiers that lived and worked in the area. The Mississippi bubble burst in France as Pierre made his way to the New World.

❧

Life back in France was in a state of flux. Francois, Marie, and Landis made a safe journey home. Life was never going to be the same for any of the Mayeuxes, though. Even Henrietta, the Mayeux housekeeper, had passed.

"The house is so quite without Pierre here," said Marie to Francois as they settled in the drawing room after supper only weeks after Pierre's departure.

"Our nest is left with only us two old birds. I think I will get a glass of brandy," said Francois. "Do you want one?" Francois already knew the answer. Marie hardly ever drank brandy, except maybe on Christmas.

"No, I can sleep just fine without brandy. And don't call me an old bird," said Marie snickering.

"That's the first time I have heard you laugh in days. I received a letter from Emily today. She warned us about a financial crisis looming. Leon heard rumors that John Law is considering abandoning the banknote completely. Henri and I discussed what to do with all those banknotes we still have from the sale of our Mississippi Company stock," said Francois.

"What have you decided?" asked Marie.

"Well, we discussed several options, but we have not made a final decision. We thought about purchasing land, but we wouldn't be able to buy much because most people consider the notes near worthless. We thought about buying another business but all we know is tax farming. We have been exchanging the notes for coins from our tax receipts but hardly anyone is paying taxes with coins these days. Or we could just hold on to them and use them as fire starters. I foresee sparse times ahead for our tax farm, Marie."

"Francois, you always worry too much. We still have the income from our farming ground. And you have that large stash of gold and silver coins hidden somewhere. Our home and land are debt free. We will be just fine. God will provide," said Marie.

"You have always been my temperance and fortitude, Marie. Have you heard anything lately from the Beniots and that damned Simone?"

"As a matter of fact, I have some news. I was waiting for the right time to tell you. Simone is pregnant! She came over to the house yesterday morning and told me herself."

"Damn it, I spilled some brandy. What did you say? Pregnant?" said Francois. He poured himself a second glass.

"I must write Pierre and inform him," said Marie.

"I don't know if that's a good idea. He may take it upon himself to return to France and ruin his whole plea bargain. Let's give it some time. Time resolves all uncertainty."

"These damned banknotes," said Regent Philippe II, Duke of Orleans. "They are worthless. They are floating around my kingdom everywhere and the creator is nowhere to be found. Where is John Law?"

"Last I heard he was on holiday with Princess Anna at Versailles," said Minister Dubois.

"He has such bad taste," said Regent Philippe.

"As your tutor, I taught you everything I know, Philippe, but unfortunately I was not skilled in finance. But I do know that John Law is not a friend of France. His only concern is John Law. Philippe, the Crown must take some action. The estates are fed up. There are riots in the streets in Paris. Priests and bishops tell me that the faithful have stopped tithing. Nobles have lost everything. Minsters of the Navy, Toulouse, Pontchartrain and d'Armenonville are having difficulty paying and retaining soldiers. The Louisiana colony has become an extravagant drain on the royal treasury. I am afraid that John Law has created a Mississippi bubble ready to burst."

"What do you propose we do?" asked Philippe.

"If we allow this malaise to continue, France will go bankrupt. John Law must be sacked," said Minister Dubois.

"But John is my friend. We will have the Parlement de Paris execute judgment," said Philippe. "Contact Magistrate Perrot with the *Chambre des Enquêtes* to handle the inquest. He owes me a favor."

"We have contracted a spell of the calms," said Pierre from the deck of the *La Profond*.

"Is that a stomach disease?" asked Marie. Pierre and Adrien laughed.

"No," said Adrien. "The barometric pressure is not changing so there are no winds. We had a dead calm throughout the night. Look at the smooth sea this morning. The ship drifts aimlessly."

"It looks like a sheet of glass. Will we get lost?" asked Marie. "We lost sight of land so many days ago."

"No, we won't get lost. The captain has been much more vigilant than us. I rose early and have been watching him take readings on the hour," said Adrien.

"Look at that sunrise and the soft blue sky. At least we are pointed west. I guess we sit and wait until the winds return. In the meantime we can enjoy this clear and beautiful day," said Pierre.

"I did learn some things about the weather during my studies," said Marie. Adrien got up and walked along the deck to join officers talking about the weather.

"Where did you study?" asked Pierre, happy to be alone with Marie.

"I was tutored at home and then entered the Université Paris-Sorbonne. I was matriculating there until Father decided to pursue this new life in the Louisiana colony."

"Why would he leave a comfortable life in France?" asked Pierre.

"Things became difficult for him. His family is from nobility. He was of the *Noblesse Militaire*. His grandfather was bestowed nobility after a succession of Selliers held military commands. Father fought in the War of the Spanish Succession and rose from a distinguished line of military officers. They fought in the Franco-Spanish War,

Franco-Dutch War and the Nine Years' War. But he experienced a financial setback. He fully invested in stock of the Mississippi Company and made all the wrong moves. He was buying when he should have been selling and selling when he should have been buying. He lost everything, our land, our home, our nobility," said Marie as she sobbed. "He had to beg for the deputy intendant position with the Company. Mother had apprehensions about coming to the Louisiana colony. I could not let her come alone."

"Looks like we have the Mississippi Company to thank for putting you and me together," said Pierre with a smile. He comforted Marie with a hug.

"Pierre, Marie, come quickly. Someone died last night!" shouted Adrien.

"Who was it?" asked Pierre.

"A passenger on our deck. She died in her sleep," said Adrien.

Pierre made his way to a group of people gathered around the body, brought to the top deck by a crewman. Word was beginning to spread throughout the ship. The wailing husband of the deceased was causing a commotion among some of the passengers.

"What's going on?" asked Captain Pemanech as he approached.

"My wife died last night. She was not feeling well the last few days. I woke up this morning and she was dead."

"What is her name and where are you from?" asked the captain.

"Her name is Marianne Roussel. We are from Troyes in Champagne Province," said Mr. Roussel.

"We are still over thirty days from the Louisiana colony. If we were closer to our destination, I would allow you to bury her in the New World. But I must insist that we bury her at sea," said the captain. "The sail maker will prepare the body and Father Robillard will perform a short service thirty minutes before dinner."

"Burial at sea is the proper method of disposing of a body from a ship at sea," said Adrien as the crowd began to disperse. "I remember one voyage, the ship's captain decided to hold the body until we could find a land cemetery. Poor fellow decomposed something awful, and the stench invaded our sleeping quarters."

"I would sure hate to become fish food," said Marie.

"If you were planted into the ground, you would become worm food," said Pierre. "Death is an unpleasant experience anywhere you die. She died peacefully in her sleep. Some die horrible deaths."

"The most important thing with death is whether your soul is prepared," said Marie. "Is your soul prepared, Pierre?"

"I'm not quite sure," said Pierre. "How do you know?"

"If you don't know, then you are not prepared," said Marie. "I guess I will have to teach you one day."

"I've always been told that an albatross carries the souls of dead sailors to heaven," said Adrien. Marie and Pierre looked puzzled.

"That is preposterous," said Marie in English.

"Her body will be stitched into a piece of canvas and a couple of thirty-six pound cannonballs will be placed at her feet to prevent her from floating or finding her way to shore," said Adrien. "Tradition has it that the last stitch of the sailmaker's needle passes through her nose to satisfy everyone that she is actually dead."

"That's disgusting. Let's meet back at the top deck at 11:30 for the burial service. I need to tell Mother and Father," said Marie.

At 11:30, drums and bells announced the solemnity of the hour. Most everyone on the ship gathered on the top deck to pay their last respects. Mr. Roussel was having a hard time with his wife's death. He was crying uncontrollably. But the sun was shining brightly and the top deck was hot. The wind had not resumed. A large crowd had assembled around the body.

"We gather here today to remember the life of Marianne Roussel," said Captain Pemanech. "She and her husband are from Troyes of the Champagne Province in France. She was an engage of the Dartaguiette concession in the Louisiana colony. Unfortunately, she succumbed to one of the many perils in sea travel. Father Robillard, if you will."

"In the name of the Father, the Son and the Holy Ghost. In this uncertain world, we can be sure of one thing: we cannot cheat death. God has decided, in his infinite wisdom, to call home his beloved daughter, Madame Roussel. Not one of us knows our fate as we journey to the Louisiana colony, but with Christ as our guide and the Holy Spirit in our heart, we can be assured that when our time to be called home arrives, God will lead the way. And now let us say prayers for our beloved sister. Our Father, who art in Heaven, hallowed be thy name, thy kingdom come, thy will be done on earth as it is in heaven. Give us this day our daily bread; forgive us our sins as we forgive those who sin against us, and lead us, not into temptation but deliver us from the evil one. Amen. Hail Mary, full of grace, the Lord is with thee. Blessed art thou among women and blessed is the fruit of thy womb, Jesus. Holy Mary, mother of God, pray for us sinners, now and at the hour of our death. Amen. God, we commend this worthy soul into your hands," said Father Robillard. He made the sign of the cross over her body and sprinkled her with Holy water. Two of the crew tipped her body from the gangplank into the sea, feet first.

"If you don't do something soon, we will have a revolution on our hands," said the regent.

"I have tried everything," said John Law. "I cannot seem to reduce the number of banknotes in circulation. I stopped printing banknotes months ago and the public has lost confidence in the value of trade in the Louisiana colony so I cannot stop the slide of share prices of the Mississippi Company. I now see that we should have backed up the banknotes with gold and silver from the outset. But in theory this system should have worked."

"France was not a good place to test your theories. This paper you have created is not worth the ink you have printed on it," said the regent. "My subjects have lost complete confidence in the Crown. And at the moment, I wear the Crown. I should have you turned over to the mobs. Maybe they would receive some satisfaction. I know I would."

"Philippe, please don't be angry with me. All of this was done to benefit you, France, and the colony. Unfortunately for us, the damned Louisiana colony did not produce the gold and silver the Spaniards are receiving from their colony in the south. The Company has already returned the royal bank and the royal mint to the Crown. I think our only alternative at this point is to abandon the banknote altogether."

"What!" cried the regent. "The banknote has nothing to do with the profitability of the Company. The banknote was your idea."

"This is my plan. The high denomination notes should be redeemed first at 10 percent of face value starting on October 1. These notes will remain legal tender for debts and taxes. The smaller denominated notes shall remain legal tender for trading purposes, but all notes will be taken out of circulation by May 1, 1721."

"And what about the Mississippi Company? Should we sell our colony to the Spaniards?" asked the regent.

"God forbid, no," said Law. "The Company would be profitable but for the losses of Company. I will try my hardest to save the Mississippi Company. The worst thing that could happen is that we are forced to get bankruptcy protection and reorganize."

"And how do you propose we implement this plan? By edict of the Crown? I think not. My subjects hate me already. You got me into this mess and you will get me out. You will sell this new proposal directly to *le Parlement de Paris* and hope they don't chop your head off in the process. Have the nobles of the Crown send this recommendation back to me as a new initiative. By the way, how are Madame Law and the children?" asked the regent.

"They are fine. They have sought refuge at the estate of the Duke de Bourbon. I've been sneaking out of your palace at night to visit her after the mobs leave," said Law. "A most terrible situation."

"How do we know that Pierre is the father of Simone's child?" asked Francois as he and Marie sat outside their home, under a large oak tree.

The coldness of the winter in northern France had fully receded and the gentle breezes of late summer were refreshing in the cool of the shade. The fields of barley and wheat were striving for maturity. Harvest time was not far off.

"Francois, she is only a child herself. Pierre was her first and only lover. She told me as much. I know in my heart that she is bearing our grandchild," said Marie.

"Well, I don't like the idea of rewarding the consequences of the defiance of my demands," said Francois.

"Since Henrietta died, I have been struggling to manage the household. Henrietta, bless her soul. She was the most dedicated and hardworking housekeeper we ever had. She was a friend. I miss her extremely. But I need help, even with Pierre gone. I miss Pierre intolerably. Companionship would be good for me. You are always working."

"Don't tell me what I am thinking you are going to tell me," said Francois.

"Francois, Simone is having a very difficult pregnancy. She has morning sickness and her ankles and feet are swollen. Her mother and father are always in the fields this time of year. Maybe she could stay here and help around the house and I could take care of her through her pregnancy? She is carrying your grandchild, you know," said Marie.

"So she claims. Marie, you know how much I frowned upon Pierre because of his relationship with that girl. She knew my disapproval even more than Pierre did. Now you want me to reward her for her disobedience. And she is personally responsible for Pierre's departure. She will have no respect for me and think me a fool," said Francois.

"No, she will not! I had a long talk with her. She is a smart girl. Francois, she told me about the two sets of books. She knew what you were up to from the start. She never told Pierre about your ruse. She let him go to the colony to save his life. You owe her much more than a mere one thousand livres. And in worthless banknotes! You should be ashamed!"

Chapter Fourteen

"What day is it today?" asked Pierre as Marie woke him from a deep sleep in his hammock. The only thing he could remember from his dreams was land. He didn't know if it was land in France or land in the Louisiana colony. But land was on everyone's mind.

"It is Sunday," said Marie. "Day number fifty-nine. We have Mass at nine o'clock this morning before dinner. Don't you like that Mass is mandatory for the crew? Even those at their post must listen in."

"I never really thought about it that much," said Pierre.

"I take pleasure in the Mass on the deck," said Marie. "All can participate—passengers and even crew at their stations. The captain told us at supper last night that those crew who don't attend Mass are given six lashes."

"Is that like a penance or a sentence?" said Pierre.

"Are you being sarcastic or are you just in a foul mood this morning?" asked Marie.

"I guess I just miss my family. The monotony and confinement on this ship is almost worse than the prison cell I shared with those vagabonds in Amiens. Thank God for you."

"Come, Pierre, let's walk the deck. Did you attend Mass every Sunday in France?"

"Yes, Mother and Father made me attend most Sundays, except those Sundays when Father would have us work in the tax farm or I had something better to do. Why?"

"We attend church faithfully every Sunday. Mother and I often attend during the week also. I hear we will be treated to a baptism at sea this morning before Mass."

"Not again. These poor souls are too stupid to say that this is not their first crossing. I haven't seen one yet sit on the pole hanging over that barrel full of water and make an offering of money to the crew. I think only one gave money. All the rest said it was their first crossing and got dunked. They are mostly engages for the Dartaguiette concession. Poor Dartaguiette."

"Lying is a sin, Pierre. But I guess a little lie wo w uldn't hurt. The passengers do seem to appreciate the ceremony. The Jesuits don't like it because they see it as a mockery of baptism. It's only a fun pastime to me," said Marie.

"Where is Adrien?" asked Pierre.

"Good morning my friend. Mademoiselle Sellier. We just saw a ship in the distance. The sail was seen on our starboard side, too distant to make out what she was, even with a spy glass; there are pirate ships in these waters. The English will board French ships and plunder all passengers and crew if they are brave enough to face our cannons," said Adrien.

"How about you, Adrien, do you attend church much?" asked Marie, unworried about piracy, except maybe for the devil stealing their souls.

"I attend church every Sunday, especially since Mother disappeared. I think she ran off with a Huguenot. Damned Protestants, I hate Protestants."

"Adrien," said Marie. "We are to love our neighbor as ourselves."

"Luckily I never had any Huguenots living next door to me," said Adrien.

"Come boys, I think we all need to attend Mass this morning."

"That is a good idea. One of the rules on ship is that everyone must be on time for Mass, or lose their rations for a day. If you miss Mass, the penalty is even worse—lashes," said Adrien.

"So I have heard," said Pierre.

After several passengers were baptized at sea, the chaplain appeared for the Mass on the top deck. He opened the Mass as usual, read a couple of chapters from the Bible, led the congregation in hymns, consecrated the host, and distributed the Eucharist. A few of the passengers were noticeably impressed by the service. For others, the ritual was novel and bizarre; they never got to church much on shore.

After Mass, some of the officers of the ship played the harpsichord and bass while the passengers listened to the music. Some of the sailors danced on the quarterdeck, and others sang. Some of the passengers and crew played cards or chess, but not for money, because it was forbidden on the ship. After dinner, all settled down for a nap, except of course the crew on duty. The sky was sunshine blue and the wind was strong. The ship rolled with the huge swells of the ocean as the sails fluttered with the gusts of wind.

"Mother is sea sick again. I don't think dinner agreed with her," said Marie.

"I don't think these seaman's rations are working out for me. I am sick of them. Any treat from the captain's table today?" asked Pierre.

"I did manage a piece of chicken. The captain informed us that we are officially out of fresh meat. The cook killed the last of the livestock on board. We will be eating salted meat and fish until the end of the voyage," said Marie.

"Pierre, Marie, come quick," shouted Adrien. "Look—birds!"

Pierre and Marie hugged. "Birds can only mean land is near."

At that moment, bells and drums sounded. The ship was on full watch with all crew on deck.

"What's going on?" asked Marie.

"I am not sure," said Adrien. He ran down an officer he had befriended and asked.

"The crew in the crow's nest sighted dark clouds on the horizon. The captain thinks it might be a hurricane," said the officer. "It is south of us. We are going to try and outrun it."

"What is a hurricane?" asked Marie

"A powerful storm with fierce winds. I read about them preparing for the voyage. It's a Spanish word. *Ce n'est pas bon*," said Pierre.

"The winds in a hurricane rotate counter clockwise. Notice how these strong easterlies are pulling us due west. We will definitely reach land faster, but this damned hurricane might suck us in," said Adrien. "Look—I can see the dark clouds in the southern horizon already."

"What should we do?" asked Marie.

"What can we do but trust the captain, and of course, pray," said Adrien.

The later the day progressed, the cloudier the skies became until the sun completely disappeared. Light rain began to fall with violent qualls of intense wind every so often. Water began to seep into the between decks where all of the passengers had gathered. The constant howling wind rattled the closed cannon hole covers as the last remaining light in the between decks was slowly extinguished by the setting sun. Sailing into a hurricane was dangerous, but sailing into one at night could be suicide. Everyone was exhausted from the voyage and all wanted to reach land as soon as possible—but at what cost? Marie told her parents that she was going to ride out the storm with Pierre.

"Mother insisted on a bundling board, but I convinced her that the ship lacked one. We are headed to a New World anyway, and a board between us in a hammock would be impossible," said Marie, hoping that Pierre's embrace would comfort her.

The fear produced by the ferocity of the beast would often cloud the mind. But with the Holy Spirit present, fear of the future seemed to wane. Confusion became clearer knowing that salvation was within reach. Life on this Earth was but a journey to a New World with the expectation of a rendezvous with wisdom along the way. Wisdom revealed truth and true certainty of a person's final destination. Rest on the *La Profond,* though, at least temporarily, was going to be impossible.

"I am going top deck to see if I can lend a hand," said Adrien. "I cannot sleep."

"Are you crazy? Don't fall overboard," shouted Pierre as Adrien scampered up the stairs. "Come, Marie, crawl into my hammock," he said as the hammock rocked to and fro with the rolling of the ship. Lightning flashes would every so often illuminate the beauty and fear in Marie's face, but Pierre felt pure bliss when the thunder crashes caused her to hug him even tighter.

There was not much sleep for anyone on the *La Profond*. The captain ordered all hands on deck for the entire night. Rain poured from the skies as squall lines thrust and battered the ship through the darkness. Water seeped through the top deck. All the passengers and their luggage were soaked. The sailors stayed busy throughout the night hoisting and lowering sails, pumping water from the hold, and stitching torn sails. The captain struggled to keep the ship headed west, northwest as the northeast winds of the hurricane in its northern quadrant pushed the ship along. Yet, the strain on the ship's structure with each pounding wave loosened her bones. Adrien helped man the pump most of the night.

"Wake up you lovebirds. Land has been spotted. The captain thinks we have reached Puerto Rico," said Adrian.

Pierre and Marie had gotten little sleep but that didn't matter. Their bond had grown stronger. They were drenched from the seeping rain, but the idea of land was refreshing news. A buzz about land was about the ship.

"What about the hurricane?" asked Pierre.

"The captain managed to outrun it. We are still north of it but at a safe distance. The captain intends to make a run for CapFrançais, the capitol of Saint-Dominique. It's French territory. Come topside," said Adrien.

"Let's get up, Pierre," said Marie. "I cannot wait any longer. It's been sixty-two days since we left France. I must see land again."

"Hold on. I kind of like laying here with you," said Pierre.

"Oh, Pierre," said Marie, getting up from the hammock and climbing to the top deck. "Come and see the blue and turquoise waters," she hollered. "Isn't this beautiful? And these big, white, fluffy clouds hanging so low look like angels dancing on a sheet of blue silk. And look, porpoises!"

"Land ahoy! Can you see it on the horizon, Marie?" asked Pierre as he came to stand beside her. "That must be an island of the Bahamas. I also see a darkness south of us. That hurricane seems to be following us like some malevolent force."

"The captain said this island is Puerto Rico, a Spanish colony," said Adrien.

In his mind, Pierre said a silent prayer for his safety and that of his two new friends in the New World. He wasn't sufficiently comfortable to pray out loud, but his newly strengthened religious beliefs, brought about by Marie and the ocean crossing, moved him to prayer.

"Look at those trees that look like inverted chicken feet," said Marie.

"Those are palm and coconut trees," said Adrien. "The coconuts are filled with a sweet milky liquid and the flesh is good to eat. I ate some on my first voyage to the Antilles a year ago. Coco is a Spanish term meaning skull. When you peel off the outer husk, a face appears at one end with a nose and two eyes," said Adrien.

"The white sand beaches are beautiful," said Marie.

"The captain is trying to get us to CapFrançais before the hurricane gets there," said Adrien. "God save the king."

An air of excitement brewed on the top deck as passengers began to emerge. Everyone was drying out clothing. Some crew members played their instruments as others sang along. The rays of the sun peaked over the eastern horizon, energizing the humid salty air. Even the sea gulls sang along as the *La Profond* skirted the coastline of Puerto Rico.

Santo Domingo, comprising all of the island of Hispaniola, became the first Spanish colony in the Americas after it was discovered by Christopher Columbus in 1492. Columbus's first landfall in the New World was on an island he named San Salvador in the Bahamas. The Spanish conquistadors enslaved the indigenous Tainos on the Bahamas. An estimated thirty thousand Tainos inhabited the Bahamas at the time of Christopher Columbus's arrival. Eventually, the Spanish transported much of the Tainos population to Hispaniola for use as forced labor. The slaves suffered from harsh conditions and most died from contracting diseases to which they had no immunity; half of the Taino died from smallpox alone. The indigenous population of the Bahamas and Hispaniola was severely diminished.

The Bahamas were largely abandoned by the Spanish during the 1500s and control of the islands rotated between the French, British, and Spanish during the 1600s. In 1703, a joint Franco-Spanish expedition briefly occupied the Bahamian capital during the War of the Spanish Succession. During proprietary rule, the Bahamas became a haven for pirates, including the infamous Blackbeard (*ca.* 1680–1718). The Bahamas became a British Crown colony in 1718, when the British clamped down on piracy.

Christopher Columbus was the first to bring sugarcane to the Caribbean during his second voyage to the Americas, initially to the island of Hispaniola. Sugarcane was native to the tropical regions of South Asia. European indigo from Asia arrived through ports in Portugal, the Netherlands, and England. Many sugarcane and indigo plantations were established by all the European powers in these tropical climates.

Unable to use a diminished native population for forced agricultural labor, the Spanish settlers on Hispaniola began to import captive Africans. This was the beginning of the Atlantic slave trade. The first Africans were sold as slaves in Santo Domingo (at the time, the entire island of Hispaniola) in 1520. Slavery was not a major institution in the early Spanish colony. This was because Santo Domingo was not a very successful colony. After the gold deposits were exhausted, the focus of the Spanish moved west and south to Central and South America.

Only a small number of Spaniards remained, perhaps a few thousand. And many of those were the children of Spanish fathers and Taino mothers.

The principal economic activity became livestock. Columbus had introduced cattle and pigs to the island. Many escaped and ran wild, and they multiplied. The Spanish settlers began raising livestock. There was a ready market. The Spanish ships sailing by the island en route to Mexico and Panama stopped in Santo Domingo for supplies. Few slaves were needed to support this livestock economy.

The western part of Hispaniola changed the slave trade when the French began settling the small island of La Tortue off the northwestern coast of Hispaniola. La Tortue attracted smugglers, run-away indentured servants, and European sailors who had jumped ship. At first, they operated within the law, capturing livestock on Hispaniola to sell for leather and meat. Gradually, they became more adventuresome, and rather than trading with European ships, especially the Spanish, they began seizing their ships. La Tortue thus became an infamous pirate den. The Spanish treasure ships offered rich booty. Many notorious pirates, such as Olivier Levasseur (Oliver La Buse), operated from La Tortue or recruited crews there, including the famous British pirate Henry Morgan.

The French dispatched colonists to settle La Tortue and the northwestern coast of Hispaniola and named its possession on the island of Hispaniola, Saint-Domingue (now Haiti). CapFrançais, later known as the "Paris of the Antilles," became the capital of Saint-Domingue. The Spanish, with only a small population on Hispaniola, decided to abandon the western end of the island to the French. This left it to the French to "domesticate" the pirates. Recalcitrant pirates were hanged. To those willing to change their ways, the French offered inducements. Women in French jails, mostly accused of prostitution or thievery, were deported to the island. As a result, the western third of Hispaniola became a French colony. The French exploring and settling on the main island succeeded in largely displacing the Spanish from western Hispaniola. One of Louis XIV's wars in Europe eventually demanded the Spanish to cede western Hispaniola to the French under the Treaty of Ryswick (1697).

Fabulous wealth was generated in the island colony. The wealth was derived primarily from cane sugar. The French began transforming the colony into a vast sugarcane plantation. The French began importing large numbers of African slaves to work the plantations. Some of the plantations were huge, employing thousands of slaves. The destruction of the Taino and importation of Africans changed the demographics of Saint-Domingue. In the 1700s, it became the richest colony in the Americas.

Saint-Domingue was dedicated to the production of sugar— a commodity of unprecedented value. Its exports were more valuable to France than all of the thirteen American colonies were to Great Britain. Saint-Domingue was the largest producer of sugar in the world. Eventually, cattle, coffee, indigo, and spice plantations were formed. Nicknamed the "Pearl of the Antilles," Saint-Domingue became the richest and most prosperous French colony in the West Indies, cementing its status as an important port in the Americas for goods and products flowing to and from France and Europe.

The first sugar windmill was built in 1685. The labor for these mills was provided by African slaves. The slaves who arrived came from hundreds of different tribes, their languages often mutually incomprehensible. The majority came from Senegal and the Congo. To regulate slavery, in 1685 King Louis XIV of France enacted the Code Noir (the Black Code), which accorded certain human rights to slaves and responsibilities to their masters, who were obliged to feed, clothe, and provide for the general well-being of their slaves. It was ratified by Louis XIV and adopted by the Saint-Domingue sovereign council in 1687. It was later applied in the Louisiana colony in 1724. The second version of the code was codified by Louis XV when he was thirteen years old, in 1724. In sixty articles, the document specified the following:

Jews could not reside in the French colonies (Art. 1). Slaves must be baptized in the Roman Catholic Church (Art. 2). Public exercise of any religion other than Roman Catholicism was prohibited; masters who allowed or tolerated it by their slaves could also be punished (Art. 3). Only Catholic marriages would be recognized (Art. 8). White men could be fined for having children with slave concubines owned by another man, as would the slave concubine's master. If the man who engaged in sexual relations with a slave was the master of the slave concubine, the slave and any resulting children would be removed from his ownership. If a free, unmarried man should have relations with a slave owned by him, he should then be married to the slave concubine, thus freeing her and any resulting child from slavery (Art. 9). Weddings between slaves must be carried out only with the master's permission (Art. 10). Slaves must not be married without their own consent (Art. 11). Children born between married slaves were also slaves, belonging to the female slave's master (Art. 12). Children between a male slave and a free woman were free; children between a female slave and a free man were slaves (Art. 13). Slaves must not carry weapons except under permission of their masters for hunting purposes (Art. 15). Slaves belonging to different masters must not gather at any time under any circumstance (Art. 16). Slaves should not sell sugarcane, even with permission of their masters (Art. 18). Slaves should not sell any other commodity without permission of their masters (Art. 19-21). Masters must give food (quantities specified) and clothes to their slaves, even to those who were sick or old (Art. 22-27). Slaves could not testify at trial but only give information (Art. 30-32). A slave who struck his or her master, his wife, mistress or children could be executed (Art. 33). A slave husband and wife (and their prepubescent children) under the same master were not to be sold separately (Art. 47). Fugitive slaves absent for a month should have their ears cut off and be branded. For another month, their hamstring would be cut and they would be branded again. A third time, they would be executed (Art. 38). Free blacks who harbored fugitive slaves would be beaten by the slave owner and fined three hundred pounds of sugar per day of refuge given; other free people who harbored fugitive slaves would be fined ten livres per day (Art. 39). A master who falsely accused a slave of a crime and had the slave put to death could be fined (Art. 40). Masters may chain and beat slaves but may not torture nor mutilate them (Art. 42). Masters who killed their slaves could be punished (Art. 43). Slaves were community property and could not be mortgaged, and must be equally split between the master's inheritors, but could be used as payment in case of debt or bankruptcy, and otherwise sold (Art. 44-46, 48-54). Slave masters of twenty years of age (twenty-five years without parental permission) may free their slaves (Art. 55). Slaves who were declared to be sole legatees by their masters, or named as executors of their wills, or tutors of their children, should be held and considered as freed slaves (Art. 56). Freed slaves were French subjects, even if born elsewhere (Art. 57). Freed slaves had the same rights as French colonial subjects (Art. 58, 59). Fees and fines paid with regard to the Code Noir must go to the royal administration, but one third would be assigned to the local hospital (Art. 60).

Slavery was introduced by the French colonists in Louisiana in 1706, when they made raids on the Chitimacha settlements. Thousands of indigenous people were killed, and the surviving women and children were taken as slaves. The enslavement of natives, including the Atakapa, Bayogoula, Natchez, Choctaw, Chickasaw, Taensa, and Alabamon, would continue throughout the history of French rule. While Native American Indians had sometimes made slaves of enemies captured in war, they also tended to adopt them into their tribes and incorporate them among their people.

The French introduced African slaves to the Louisiana colony in 1710, after capturing a number as plunder during the War of the Spanish Succession. Trying to develop the new Louisiana territory, the French transported more than two thousand Africans to New Orleans between the years 1717 and 1721 on at least eight ships owned by the Mississippi Company. These slaves originated from French and Spanish colonial territories in Africa.

During the 1600s, the popularity of coffee increased in Europe. Previously, coffee imported into Europe had come from the Arabian Peninsula, over which none of the European nations had any control. Dutch spies successfully managed to smuggle a coffee plant out of Yemen. These new plants soon found their way into the Caribbean. The French in Martinique successfully cultivated the coffee plant. Coffee was soon adopted by the locals. Within three years, coffee plantations spread all over Martinique and to the neighboring islands of Saint-Domingue and Guadeloupe. Coffee production became successful in the Caribbean, but never as successful as sugarcane.

Chapter Fifteen

"Land ahoy," shouted a crew member from the crow's nest. All of the passengers were on the top deck gawking at the large island on the horizon. The crew began singing the *Te Deum* and many of the passengers joined them. Yet the pristine, natural beauty of the New World scowled at the interlopers as if protected by a beast of nature. The festive atmosphere was dampened as the passengers recognized they were not welcomed guests. The darkness in the west was easily visible over the open ocean. The outer clouds of the approaching hurricane began to slowly conceal the morning sun. The rocking boat from the increasingly turbulent sea tossed the passengers about the deck like falling chess pieces. But, finally, the *La Profond* entered the beautiful deep-water harbor of Cap-Français on the north side of the island.

"The Spanish own the other end of the island. This end of the island is called Saint-Domingue," said Pierre.

"The harbor is filled with ships. I assume they are seeking shelter from the storm," said Marie.

"They are from all parts of the world," said Adrien. "Look at their flags. There is a Dutch ship and several French ships. I have seen several Spanish ships. There is a damned Union Jack," shouted Adrien in disgust.

BANG!

"What was that?" asked Marie.

"The captain ordered a single shot of a twenty-pounder as an emergency announcement of our arrival," said Adrien.

"I hope that that British ship doesn't start shooting back at us," joked Marie.

"Look, the crew in the rigging are rolling up the large main mast sails to slow the ship's forward speed," said Pierre.

"You are becoming quite a good sailor," said Marie.

"Only the mizzen sails in the rear will remain," said Adrien. "Those smaller sails are much more maneuverable in this increasing wind speed from the hurricane. We will probably anchor in the harbor a safe distance from shore."

"Heave–ho, heave–ho," cried the sailors in unison as they lowered a heavy anchor to drag along the bottom to slow the forward speed of the ship. The crew was quickly at work removing all of the rigging, not just the sails. They were being tossed around on the main mast by the gusts of wind and the rolling ship. Two first lieutenants were walking the top deck making announcements to the passengers. "Prepare to disembark. Leave all of your luggage; take only bare necessities. Meet at muster stations," they shouted.

"I must find Mother and Father," stated Marie with alarm.

"Meet me back at the foot of the main mast before you get off this ship," hollered Pierre as panic began to set in among the passengers.

He went to his sleeping quarters and was followed by the two lieutenants with their announcements. He managed to stuff one of the smaller bags of silver coins given to him by his father in his pocket, never thinking about his mother and father back home. Marie was in his thoughts. Leaving his meager possessions behind, Pierre hurriedly returned to the top deck to rendezvous with her. Adrien was waiting at the main mast but there was no Marie.

"Have you seen Marie?" asked Pierre.

"No, but this wind is getting stronger. This rain is stinging my face," said Adrien.

The wind was so violently strong that the coconut trees were bending to and fro as if dancing with one another as each squall of rain passed through, followed by another every few minutes. The crew was busy at work. Some were taking down all the remaining sails and rigging. Others were lowering all of the anchors, hoping that the wind would not push their only means of transportation into the shoreline. Two medium-sized cannons were brought from the hold. The crew tied ropes to one and threw it overboard in front of the ship and were working on the second one for additional anchorage in the rear as Marie walked up, arguing with her mother.

"I want you to stay with us," said Madame Sellier.

"But Mother, Father will be tending to you. Pierre will keep me safe," argued Marie.

"I will not let her out of my sight," said Pierre as he interrupted in an attempt to pacify Madame Sellier's concerns for Marie. Madame Sellier, in her hysteria, finally capitulated.

"Muster station number one, prepare to disembark," shouted a lieutenant as the *La Profond's* only dinghy bounced alongside her. Guests at the captain's table, the priests, dignitaries, and merchants made up the group at muster station one. Marie clung to Pierre as Monsieur and Madame Sellier were pushed toward the escape hatch in the gunwale by a sailor. They joined the other first class passengers climbing down the ten-foot-wide Jacob's ladder hanging on the side of the ship into the awaiting dinghy, without Marie.

"Look, tenders are coming from shore. They are much bigger than this dinghy," shouted Adrien over the howling of the wind and wailing of the women.

"These winds are getting stronger and stronger. I can't believe nature can produce such ferocity and wrath. Have you ever been through a hurricane?" Pierre asked Adrien.

"No. We get to experience this for the first time together," said Adrien. He and Pierre's friendship had blossomed during their two months together at sea. Even though their education and family upbringings were so different, they were both pioneers in spirit. Pierre gazed into the future, and Adrien answered to the present. Their personalities complimented each other and their bond was like a sapling that would eventually grow into a majestic and towering oak.

"Let's take the first tender to shore. With these increasing winds, I am afraid for the safety of the last to get off this ship," said Pierre.

"The captain and some of the crew will probably stay onboard the ship throughout the storm. God bless them," said Adrien.

"Let's go," said Marie. "I am ready to get rid of these sea legs and walk on hard ground again."

"Pardon me. Pardon me. We have Monsieur and Madame Sellier's daughter to escort to shore," shouted Adrien as they pushed through the crowded deck. The lieutenant whom Adrien had befriended allowed the three to the front of the line.

"Pierre, I don't know if I can climb down this rope ladder with the ship rocking so," said Marie as another intense gust of wind and rain pushed through.

"Adrien and I will descend with you, one of us on each side. Just don't let go of the rope. You will do just fine," said Pierre with a pierced heart. His spirit overflowed with joy knowing that Marie placed her life in his hands, even though he was also fearful.

By the time they reached the beach, the rain was blowing sideways constantly and the wind was blowing even harder. The gales merged into one continuous and unrelenting tempest. The powerful gusts changed to sustained fury. All of the tenders survived the treacherous flight from ship to shore before the brunt of the storm arrived with its full ferocity. The captain and several of the crew stayed with the ship in case an anchor line broke or if any other emergency developed. The passengers were escorted from the beach to a church only three blocks within the town center.

"Thank God for this church. I think it's the only brick structure in this town. All the other buildings I saw were made of wood," said Marie.

"It is a beautiful church," said Pierre as they walked around looking for Monsieur and Madame Sellier. "There are too many souls inside here. It seems that most of the locals have also taken shelter here."

"Maybe I'll get married in a church like this one day," said Marie.

"Maybe," said Pierre.

"Pierre, look at those black men and women. Are they slaves?" asked Marie. "I have never seen slaves before."

"I guess they are. This is the first time for me, too."

"There is your mother. It seems she is arguing with your father," said Adrien.

"I must get out of these wet clothes. Can someone get me a dry change of clothing?" Madame Sellier asked her husband as the trio walked up.

"Mother, everyone is soaking wet and no one has their luggage. We will have to make do," said Marie.

"Thank God you arrived in safety, Marie," said Monsieur Sellier. "Your mother fell as we were rushed to the church. She became awfully disoriented."

"We will all feel dizzy for a few days," said Adrien. "Every time you stand still, the ground will feel like it is moving. That ship confuses your equilibrium terribly."

"It sounds like the winds are blowing stronger and stronger," said Monsieur Sellier. "These heightened gales shriek like incoming mortar rounds from cannon fire, one after another. It brings me back to my war days."

"Adrien and I are going to take a look outside at the storm, firsthand," said Pierre. As soon as they opened the side door of the church, they could feel its fury. The storm was flipping roof shingles as if they were a deck of playing cards, and the rain was incessant.

"Listen to the howl of the storm as it rushes through these narrow streets of Cap-Francios," shouted Adrien.

"I can hardly stand straight. I can only imagine being exposed on the beach. This sea monster would swallow us up and spit us out somewhere else," shouted Pierre. "You can feel the energy in the raw power of these gusts. I cannot believe that Mother Nature can get this angry. Let's go back inside. Hell has no fury to match this."

Agonizing fear welled up inside the passengers within the church. The potency of the raging storm could be felt throughout the shelter as it shook, rattled, and creaked. The sense of being in the storm could be likened to David facing Goliath, except this time Goliath was winning. At one point hysteria nearly set in, sustained by a complete lack of rational thought. The storm was relentless. It lasted the remainder of the day and into the evening hours. No one rested through the night, sleeping in wet clothes with no food and only the little water collected from the leaking roof. Church candles provided the only light.

The next morning, the passengers of the *La Profond* all rose in unison very early—at least those that were able to sleep. The local priest living in the rectory next door said Mass. Everyone was extremely grateful to him and even more to God that they were all safe. Thankfully, the noise had disappeared and peace had returned. Quiet was the norm again. The sun's rays streamed through the stained glass windows of the church, but the sight outside exposed the fury of the hurricane.

"My God, it is so hot," said Pierre.

"I bet I could cut this air with a knife," said Marie as the sojourners ventured out of the church and witnessed the devastation. Several members of the crew were gathered in front of the church and the first lieutenant began announcements.

"Please come forward and gather round. The *La Profond* safely weathered the storm, however, she is leaking. We are in the process of patching her and will restock her for the final leg of our journey to the Louisiana colony. The captain plans to set sail at dusk and we will start boarding two hours before. Keep account of your mates. Anyone not present at the dock will be left behind. Spread the word."

"Let's see if we can find the local intendant," said Monsieur Sellier. "I think the name of the Governor-General is Léon, Marquis de Sorel and the intendant is Jean-Baptiste Dubois Duclos or François de Montholon. Maybe he can show us some of the island."

"The destruction is so great," said Madame Sellier.

"They are probably busy, Father," said Marie as they walked through the debris lying in the streets.

"Just look at the uprooted trees. Half of the buildings have roof damage," said Pierre.

Upon arriving at the governor's quarters, they saw French soldiers were posted around the perimeter. Monsieur Sellier attempted entrance at the front gate but was informed by the guard that the governor and intendant were absent.

"Where can we hire a carriage and horses?" asked Pierre.

The guard directed them to the nearest livery. It was only blocks away, and Pierre secured an open, two-horsed carriage for four people for only one silver livre. Madame Sellier asked about a driver, and Pierre volunteered his services. Marie climbed up with Pierre into the driver's seat.

"We mustn't venture out too far," shouted Madame Sellier. "We don't know how safe it is here."

"We will take the main road out of town for a short distance to see some of the countryside," shouted Pierre over the clacking of the horses' shoes on the cobblestone street.

"I see French soldiers stationed all around town," said Marie. "I wonder if there is any looting."

"Probably. But I am sure the owners of these plantations keep their slaves under lock and key during hurricanes," said Adrien. The carriage exited town and slowed to a crawl on the muddy dirt road. "I see some of them clearing the road ahead of us."

"I feel sorry for these black Africans. I don't agree that any man should be the property of another," said Marie.

"Yes, but economics drives commerce. Who else would work these fields?" asked Pierre.

"The sugarcane crop seems to be severely damaged. Most of it is laying on the ground," said Monsieur Sellier. "Pierre, take this road to that plantation house."

A young black boy ran up to the carriage as Pierre steered the horses near the front entrance of the main house. Many of the slave quarters were severely damaged by the hurricane. Slaves were already hard at work repairing their barracks.

"*Bonjour, puis-je vous aider,*" shouted a white man who came out of the house and onto the front porch. Monsieur Seller exited the carriage.

"Bonjour, my name is Jean Sellier. We arrived on the *La Profond* yesterday rather hurriedly. We are on our way to the Louisiana colony. I was recently appointed deputy intendant there. We are just sightseeing and decided to stop at the first farm out of town."

"Welcome to L'Hermitage Plantation. I am the owner, Gaspard Delfosse. I would offer to show you around, but I am currently preoccupied. Cane harvest season is under way and we get this damned hurricane."

"I understand. Yesterday was our first encounter with the destructive forces of a hurricane. Unbelievable devastation," said Monsieur Sellier.

"Tee Boy, run and get BuhBuh. BuhBuh is one of my drivers. He will show you around a bit," said Delfosse.

"Sorry for the inconvenience of us showing up unannounced," said Pierre. "How big is the farm and how many slaves do you own?"

"Twenty leagues by fifty leagues, about one thousand arpents, and three hundred forty-nine *des esclaves*. We plant mostly sugarcane and mill it ourselves. Here's BuhBuh. BuhBuh, take these people to tour the yard. Have a safe trip to Louisiana. Sorry for my hasty departure," said Delfosse.

"Yea sir, Master. Follow me," said BuhBuh, an older black man with a muscular build who spoke good French. They immediately encountered an overseer effecting punishment on another slave. "He tried to escape during the hurricane. He will receive fifty lashes for tryin' to run away and five days in irons with bread and water. Master don't like no runaways. Most of us work the fields; only a few work as domestics in the master's house. I started in the fields."

"And now you supervise your mates?" asked Marie.

"A man got to do what a man got to do. It has its benefits. Me, my wife, and children have our own house. She works in the master's house; Tee Boy is my son. We get weekly food rations—usually corn meal, lard, meat, molasses and flour—and we have our own vegetable patch and fruit trees. I have a gun and hunt wild game," said BuhBuh proudly.

"What are your duties?" asked Monsieur Sellier.

"The plantation has two white overseer and eight black drivers. We set the work pace and direct the plowin', plantin', hoein', and pickin'. We work from sun up to sun down. Master says we must not work on Sunday. Sunday is for Christos."

"Do you command respect from your people?" asked Pierre.

"They look to me to solve their disputes. Master trusts me, so they obey me. I like peace and harmony. I am not a devil. As long as everyone does their work, I am happy," said BuhBuh. "These buildings are the barracks. They must be repaired from the storm damage because everyone sleeps here. Then it's back to work in the cane fields. Meals are cooked and eaten here in the central cookhouse by the elderly men or women who are no longer able to work in the fields. And this is our church. Surprisingly, it did not receive any damage from the storm. There yonder is the sugar mill."

"I see that your people face many hardships in bondage," said Marie.

"Well, Monsieur Delfosse is a kind master. Others fare much worse," said BuhBuh. "I must leave you now. I have many duties today and many more because of this storm. God bless."

"*Au revoir*," said Madame Sellier. "And *merci beaucoup*."

As they walked back to the carriage, Marie wondered about their future. "These conditions scare me, Pierre. The poverty and hardships of daily life here weighs on my heart," said Marie. "I can only wonder what the living conditions will be like in the Louisiana colony."

"I can nearly assure you that it will not be the comforts we enjoyed in France. But together, you and I will build a new life," said Pierre. Marie smiled with delight at that thought.

By the time the adventurers returned to town, turned in the carriage, and found a local selling native food on the road side, the day turned into late afternoon. Many of the passengers of the *La Profond* began returning to the dock to prepare for boarding. Pierre had other things on his mind.

"You all head down to the dock. Adrien and I have a mission to complete," said Pierre. Adrien didn't know what Pierre had in mind but followed along with anticipation.

"Adrien, come with me to this jeweler I saw in town. I want to purchase Marie a courtship ring," said Pierre.

"Are you still in shock from the hurricane?" asked Adrien.

"Adrien, I have extreme feelings for Marie, feelings that I never had for Simone. Unlike with Simone, we haven't made feet for children's stockings yet so I know these feelings are real. I love this girl. I cannot lose her to the Louisiana colony," said Pierre.

After the last tender reached the *La Profond*, the captain ordered the main sail unfurled. It caught one of the leftover gusts of wind from the hurricane and the ship set sail for the last leg of its voyage to the Louisiana colony in the finest weather imaginable. Dusk departed and night arrived. The sun was dosed by the refreshed ocean waves as a blanket of twinkling stars swathed the sleeping goliath. They sailed along the south coast of Cuba, which belonged to the Spaniards, with lights from the island in constant view. Jamaica and the Caymans were to the left and belonged to the English. The captain then steered a northwest course for Louisiana, often having to tack to fight the occasional northerly winds left over from the hurricane.

A Canadian by birth and operating under the patronage of King Louis XIV of France, Iberville's first journey to the most southern end of the Louisiana colony was to locate the mouth of the Mississippi River and to establish a French presence on the Gulf of Mexico to discourage Spanish and English incursions into the landmass claimed by France. The Spanish, upon learning of the plans of a permanent French settlement on the Gulf, quickly occupied Pensacola Bay. The Perdido River became the boundary that separated Spanish Florida from French Louisiana. If the English or Spanish had gained a foothold, France's lucrative fur trade from interior North America would have been in jeopardy. Iberville's original intention was to establish the first French fort in the Louisiana colony on the banks of the Mississippi River. But the river's constant overflow made it impossible to find a suitable location during his first expedition up the Mississippi River in March 1699 because of spring flooding. Upon return to Ship Island on April 7, where his fleet of ships was anchored, Iberville observed in his journal, *"an elevated place that appeared very suitable."* This area was on the mainland on the northeast shore of the Bay of Biloxi.

Iberville sounded a channel and found seven feet of water that enabled him to bring his supply barges close to shore. In his journal, he wrote that he decided to construct a fort there, as they *"could find no spot more convenient, and our provisions were failing; we could search no longer. On Wednesday, the 8th, we commenced to cut away the trees preparatory for the construction of the fort. All our men worked vigorously, and at the end of the month it was finished. In the meantime, the boats were actively engaged transporting the powder, guns, and ammunition, as well as the livestock, such as bulls, cows, hogs, fowls, turkeys, etc. . . . The fort was made with four bastions, two of them squared logs, from two to three feet thick, placed one upon the other, with embrasures for port holes, and a ditch all around. The other two bastions were stockaded with heavy timbers which took four men to lift one of them. Twelve guns were mounted."*

This first French Colonial outpost on the Gulf of Mexico was named Fort Maurepas in honor of France's Minister of the Marine, Jerome Phelypeaux de Maurepas, Count of Pontchartrain. Iberville chose the best men within the expedition to remain at the fort, including detachments of French soldiers, Canadians, and sailors to serve on the gunboats. About seventy-five people were left while Iberville returned to France on May 6, 1699. In his journal, Iberville noted that *"Sauvolle, lieutenant of a company and naval ensign of the frigate* La Marin, *was left in command as governor; Bienville* (Iberville's younger

brother), *king's lieutenant of the marine guard of the frigate* La
Badine, *was next in command. Le Vasseur, a Canadian, was ma-*
jor; de Bordenac, chaplain; M. Care, surgeon. There were besides
two captains, two cannoniers, four sailors, eighteen filibusters,
ten mechanics, six masons, thirteen Canadians and twenty sub-
officers and soldiers who comprised the garrison."

Iberville anticipated a return in early 1700. Conditions at
Fort Maurepas were generally miserable. Gnats, mosquitoes,
snakes, alligators, diseases (especially yellow fever), and the
scarcity of drinking water were prevalent. The meager crops that
were planted failed due to a severe drought. Fortunately, the
garrison was supplied by the French colony at Saint-Domingue.
Morale was low because the Canadians were accustomed to
trapping and refused to farm. Drinking of liquor was a problem.
This was the condition of the first French colonial town in the
Louisiana colony at the turn of the century.

Iberville returned to Biloxi in December 1699 with the
king's ships, the forty-six-gun frigate *Renommée* and the
seven-hundred-ton flute *Gironde*. This was joyful news to the
garrison, which had been living for more than three months on
corn. He anchored at the Biloxi Bay anchorage and delivered
supplies and provisions to his post. It was reported to him by
Governor Sauvolle that during the period, four men had died
for one reason or another. On April 26, 1700 Iberville went up
the Pascagoula River about four-and-a-half leagues and got to
the village of the Biloxis. The village was almost deserted, the nation having been destroyed by European diseases. The Indians
reported that the nation was formerly quite numerous. Iberville
returned to France in September 1700.

Upon Iberville's return to Louisiana in December of 1701,
he was informed that Commndant Sauvolle had died and
Bienville was now in command. Iberville returned with orders
from the Company to fortify Mobile Bay and he moved the
main post from Biloxi to Mobile Bay, using Dauphine Island
as a staging area for the reception of the goods and provisions

that had been brought from France. He commenced to build the Fort of St. Louis de la Mobile in 1702, about twelve leagues above the mouth of the Mobile river, on the right bank, which was the official center of the colony for the next nine years. He also met with Choctaw and Chickasaw tribal leaders hoping to develop military alliances and trade partnerships with the two Indian Nations in order to check British expansion. Iberville departed the Louisiana colony for France in April 1702 and would never return.

In 1711, a new fort was built on the bay of Mobile at the mouth of the Mobile River, known as Fort Conde. The Louisiana colony had now became a monopoly of the French merchant Antoine Crozat in 1712. Bienville served under the new governor of the colony, Antoine de la Mothe Cadillac. In 1716, Bienville commanded a military expedition that defeated the hostile Natchez Indians along the banks of the Mississippi River and as reparation, had Fort Rosalie built. Bienville once again became governor of Louisiana in 1717 when John Law appeared on the scene in France. In 1719, France warred with Spain, and Mobile was on the battlefront. As a result, Bienville decided to return the administrative capital of the Louisiana colony to the coast at the original location of Fort Maurepas further west. But due to shifting sand bars blocking harbor waters, the capital of the Louisiana colony was briefly moved to Nouveau Biloxi across Biloxi Bay from the original fort built by Iberville.

Bienville founded and began construction of La Nouvelle Orleans on May 7, 1718 on land inhabited by the Chitimacha Indians. It was named for Philippe II, Duke of Orleans, Regent of France. Bienville would eventually move the administrative capital of the Louisiana colony to La Nouvelle Orleans in 1722. The *La Profond* arrived at Nouveau Biloxi on September 16, 1720 with Bienville as commandant general.

Chapter Sixteen

"**A**re you excited about beginning a new life in the colony?" Pierre asked Marie on the top deck of the *La Profond*, under a blanket of stars.

"I never thought much about home in France during our voyage, but I am apprehensive of what the future holds," said Marie. The full moon reflecting on the ocean surface brightened her face and caused a twinkle in her eyes.

"Marie, my love for you has become like a river current—never ending," said Pierre. "Will you let me into your soul? I want to steal your heart away from your mother and father," said Pierre as he got down on one knee. "Will you marry me, Marie Sellier?"

"Yes, Pierre Mayeux. I thought you would never ask. Anyway, I don't think there will be many available men in the Louisiana colony. Be assured, you can always depend on my love for you, Pierre."

"Marie, please accept this courtship ring as a token of my love." He placed the ring on her finger, and they kissed. Pierre's breath was taken away with nervous excitement because his throbbing heart was in his throat.

"What will Mother say?" asked Marie.

"I received permission to wait on you from your father when we boarded the ship this afternoon. He fully approves." Pierre's answer relieved her, and they embraced.

After a few days of tacking contrary winds, the day of arrival was upon them. On the morning of arrival at the Louisiana colony, most passengers were up early. The sailors were busily pumping water from the hold of the ship. The temporary patch necessitated by the hurricane never stopped the leak so the passengers and crew pumped around the clock. Even Pierre and Adrien joined in the labors. Expectations were running high among the passengers because the long, difficult, and unpleasant voyage was about to end. A flurry of excitement and anticipation weaved through the top deck as a few of the employees of the Dartaguiette concession relayed the description of the Louisiana colony by Law's propaganda: brooks teeming with fish, mines full of gold, Indians to serve you hand and foot. The exhaustion from the three months at sea to Cap-Francois had burdened their will and strained their intellect. Law's propaganda provided temporary reprieve. Pierre knew better because his father and Henri had informed him of the misrepresentations used by the Mississippi Company to deceive Europeans to migrate to the colony. He told Marie and Adrien that none of these expectations were true. But they wanted to believe anyway. The mental pictures sounded of Heaven.

"Land ahoy," shouted a sailor in the crow's nest. Everyone rushed to get a glimpse of the Louisiana colony. The cool, autumn, coastal breezes were a refreshing relief from the brutal and repressive tropical heat of the islands. Singing and dancing began. The sailors started their solemn rendition of the *Te Deum laudamus*: "*We praise thee, O God; we acknowledge thee to be the Lord; all the earth doth worship thee; the Father everlasting...*" Nearly everyone joined in the rounds.

"There—there is land!" shouted Pierre who was standing on the quarterdeck with Captain De Pemanech, Monsieur Sellier, and some of the officers of the ship.

"Twelve fathoms," shouted a first lieutenant to the captain who had ordered soundings.

"Ten fathoms," shouted the first lieutenant.

"I cannot distinguish this island from any of the others on the map. We are about a league away," said Captain De Pemanech to his officers. "Deploy anchors. Dispatch the dinghy to examine the land."

When the sailors returned to the ship, the captain determined the islands were the La Chandeleur. "We are looking for Ship Island

and Nouveau Biloxi. Set sail heading due north," said Captain De Pemanech after confirming his location on his map.

Sailing north along the Isles La Chandeleur, the captain knew that he had to sail between two islands: Cat Island to the left and Horn Island to the right. Suddenly, they appeared. "That is Horn Island. It is wooded and about six leagues in length," said the captain, pointing to the right. "The Canadians who settled at Isle Dauphine put most of their cattle on the island. The cattle needed no attendance and they multiplied greatly. The Canadians grew rich even when they slept," said the captain as he let out a round of laughter. "Cat Island, so called because when it was discovered, thousands of cats were found living there. Bienville put some hogs on the island. Going to hunt, one finds only hogs in great numbers and no cats. Presumably, the hogs ate all of the cats."

"The laws of nature work in mysterious ways," said Monsieur Sellier.

"That they do. Nature is beautiful, but it can have a mean underlying quality," agreed the captain. "Nouveau Biloxi was moved from the mainland to the peninsula because the road was constantly choked with sand. Mobile and Old Biloxi are on the decline. Many of the inhabitants are moving inland to Nouvelle Orleans and further north. The soil on the coast is chiefly sand, and dry and parched. No greens can grow and the beasts are hard pressed for sustenance. And these worms from the sea attach to ships and bore holes. The merchant Marines have found that ships are not subject to attack in fresh waters."

"I see that I have much to learn in this new world," said Monsieur Sellier.

"We will drop anchor in twenty-five feet of water. Begin sounding," ordered the captain. "These larger vessels can ride safely under the island and the bottom has good holding ground. But we will attempt Biloxi Bay north of Ship Island. If choked, we will anchor off shore, exposed to the south. Prepare the dinghy to go ashore."

All eyes were on the dinghy as it landed ashore. It seemed to the passengers as if the sailors stayed for hours. Everyone watched the little boat as the sailors rowed back to the ship. Upon return of the dinghy, the captain was informed that Biloxi Bay was choked with sand and the bay could not accept the *La Profond* for anchorage.

"We will anchor in the roadstead near Ship Island. Take her in easy. Furl the main sail. Make way," shouted the captain. "Station the lookouts in the crow's nest."

"Anchors aweigh," shouted the anchor watch as bells sounded. All crew were on deck at their stations.

The ship slowly ventured to shore. A group of colonists gathered on the beach and began waving at the passengers. The passengers waved back, including Pierre, Marie, and Adrian who had gathered on the top deck.

"My mind is fleeting. I am happy that we made the crossing safely, but I have apprehensions about this place which border on fear," said Marie.

"You will be fine, Marie. I am sure Governor Bienville has accommodations for his deputy intendant. The question is, will I be able to tarry in Biloxi before heading to Law's concession at the Arkansas post?" said Pierre.

"I will insist on it," said Marie. Pierre felt somewhat relieved.

"Everyone, prepare for shore. Gather your luggage and bring it to her bows," shouted the lieutenant.

"Where is that?" asked Marie

"Top deck; starboard and port sides in the front of the ship," said Adrien.

"I never want to get on a ship again," said Marie. Adrien laughed.

By now, ship life had become old hat for most of the passengers of the *La Profond*, but everyone wanted to escape its confines. Indian and African slaves were used to unload the supplies, settlers and their luggage into packet-boats, which, in their turn, were rowed to Ship Island. The arduous first leg of their journey had finally come to an end. Now, a new chapter in the lives of all the passengers was beginning, but they were met with disorder, confusion, and mayhem on Ship Island. The island was about ten leagues from Nouvelle Biloxi. The packet-boats could not approach Biloxi nearer than one league. So smaller boats were sent to unload the packet-boats, some stranding at a distance of carbine-shot from the shore. Disembarkation was finally completed on wharfs built on the bay side of Nouvelle Biloxi. The crew managed to get everyone off of the ship safely and reacquainted them with their luggage ashore.

Nouveau Biloxi was sparsely populated, with maybe fifty colonists and as many black African and Indian slaves, with only twenty or so French soldiers. The soldiers of the new recruitment on the *La Profond* managed to find their quarters within the confines of the small fort. The new soldiers instantly became a much appreciated addition. Bienville, as governor general, was the top authority in the Louisiana colony. He was the top military leader who commanded the soldiers and maintained diplomatic relations with the Indian nations and the British and Spanish.

The second in authority was the deputy intendant (commissaire ordonnateur), a civil post. The intendant of Nouvelle France was stationed in Quebec, Canada. Intendants were the king's administrators. They oversaw justice, the police force, and finances. They managed the budget, set prices, presided over the Superior Council (the court of justice), and organized the census. Monsieur Sellier was going to become a deputy. Several small concessions lined the shore of Biloxi. White sand seemed to be the only commodity, and the land was parched. Scant wooden structures with wood bark roofs and some thatched with palmetto fronds dotted the landscape around the fort. Groves of tall pine trees marked the surrounds of Biloxi. The Dartaguiette concessionaires were met by a director of the Mississippi Company and led to their barracks.

"The colonists all seem thin and lethargic with a noticeable lack of women," stated Marie. "Maybe the women are all in their huts."

"I will not live in one of those huts," said Madame Sellier.

"Everyone seems to be scavenging for food. Those men in the shallow bay waters are digging for oysters," said Adrien.

"I am sorely disappointed with the apparent lack of food and shelter and these deplorable living conditions," said Pierre.

"Let's find the governor or the intendant," said Monsieur Sellier. "Look for the biggest house." As he was speaking, a gentleman walked up to their party.

"I heard that a ship arrived. Intendant Marc-Antoine Hubert," he said He extended a hand to Monsieur Sellier in greeting. He was then introduced to everyone.

"Deputy Intendant Jean Sellier. We have just arrived from France. We have provisions from Cap-Francois."

"This is delightful news. Any provisions are a great relief. We are always running very low on all supplies at all times. The number of resupply ships has been dwindling," said Intendant Hubert.

"Is Governor General Bienville here? I have correspondence for him from France," said Monsieur Sellier.

"No, he is at his beloved Nouvelle Orleans. He insists that it will become the capitol of the Louisiana colony. He resides there now, you know," said Intendant Hubert. "I think the capitol should be at Natchez. I just secured for myself a grant of land near Fort Rosalie at Natchez." A very awkward moment ensued.

"Well, I will deliver the news to you first," said Monsieur Sellier. "This royal edict from the Crown divides upper and lower Louisiana into nine districts: Nouvelle Orleans, Biloxi, Mobile, Alibamons, Natchez, Yazoo, Natchitoches, Arkansas, and Illinois. The intendant of New France shall remain stationed in Canada but each new district shall have its own deputy intendant. I have been appointed *commissaire ordonnateur* of Nouvelle Orleans. You shall be *commissaire ordonnateur* of Biloxi. The other deputy intendants shall follow."

Intendant Hubert was shocked with the news. He realized that his authority had just been reduced by a factor of nine. But the members of Monsieur Sellier's party erupted with shouts of joy. He had managed to keep the news secret from them all, even his wife.

"Congratulations, sir," said Pierre as Madame Sellier and Marie gave him hugs and kisses. Pierre felt a sense of relief that his future father-in-law now possessed authority in the colony and was assuming it.

"Let's take a look around this village," said Deputy Intendant Sellier.

As they approached the fort entrance, the party noticed a commotion with several people gathered. Pierre led the way and inquired.

"What's going on here?" asked Pierre of one of the bystanders.

"This Canadian is trying to sell two female Indian slaves. They were captured when Governor Bienville attacked the Chickasaw. These savages are not worth much."

"Adrien, buy the young Indian girl!" said Pierre.

"What will I do with an Indian?" asked Adrien. "And anyway, I have no funds."

"I have silver," said Pierre as he approached the Canadian. "How much do you want for the young one?"

"Ten pieces of silver," said the Canadian.

"How about five?" countered Pierre.

"She cost me that much just to keep her alive. How about seven?" said the Canadian.

"I have only six pieces of French silver," said Pierre.

"Sold," said the Canadian. He grabbed the young Indian girl's arm and pushed her toward Pierre.

"Now what will I do with an Indian slave?" asked Adrien again.

"Adrien, she knows the land; she knows the local language; she will be a tremendous asset to us. And she can probably cook," said Pierre.

"What will you name her?" asked Marie.

"Well, I've never named a person before. How about we call her Creola?" said Adrien.

"Creola. That's a fine name," said Pierre.

"Boys, I think I will have to exchange this petticoat for a pair of britches and soon," said Marie with an air of confidence for what lay ahead.

To be continued…

Made in the USA
Coppell, TX
22 November 2020